Don't miss any o...
bestselling author Debbie Macomber's
celebrated NAVY series!

"I'll be your friend, Lindy, but that's all I ever intend to be," Rush stated. He paused, his back to her. "No more kissing, Lindy. I mean that. We're going to live as brother and sister from here on out."

"Brother and sister," Lindy echoed. She knew that would last until about lunchtime tomorrow, if that long.

"And if that proves too difficult for us, I'll make arrangements to live about the *Mitchell*."

"If that's what you want," she agreed.

Rush's reaction was exactly what she'd guessed it would be. His hand slammed the counter. He whirled around to face her. "Damn it all to hell. You know it isn't!"

DEBBIE MACOMBER

NAVY Wife

Published by Silhouette Books
America's Publisher of Contemporary Romance

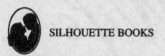 SILHOUETTE BOOKS

NAVY WIFE

ISBN 0-373-21844-3

Copyright © 1988 by Debbie Macomber

This edition published by arrangement with Harlequin Books S.A.

® and TM are trademarks of Harlequin Books S.A., used under
license. Trademarks indicated with ® are registered in the United States
Patent and Trademark Office, the Canadian Trade Marks Office and in
other countries.

Visit Silhouette at www.eHarlequin.com

Printed in U.S.A.

Dedicated to
the women behind the men
who "go down to the sea in ships."
The backbone of the Navy—the Navy wife.

Special thanks to

Sandy Campanelli,
wife of Command Master Chief John Campanelli,
USS *Nimitz*

Lee Knichel,
wife of Lieutenant Commander Ray Knichel,
USS *Nimitz*

Debbie Korrell,
wife of Chief Steven Korrell, USS *Alaska*

Rose Marie Harris,
wife of MMCM Ralph Harris, retired, U.S. Navy

Dear Reader,

I live in a navy town, across Sinclair inlet from the navy shipyard in Bremerton. Aircraft carriers, diesel submarines and destroyers are all part of the view. But growing up in eastern Washington, I didn't know many navy folk. My dad was an army man who fought in WWII, and if he talked about his war experiences, it had to do with land battles.

One thing I'll never forget is the first time I saw an aircraft carrier. I stood there agog, watching all 1092 feet of this huge flat-top sail toward Bremerton. Wives, daughters, girlfriends, sons and daughters lined the wharf. The inlet was filled with sailboats and small watercraft that zigzagged across the wake, bouncing over the swelling waves created by the *Nimitz*. As I stood on a hillside in Port Orchard and watched the scene below, I could feel the excitement and joy of the men and women aboard the carrier—and all the people waiting for them. It'd been six months since they'd seen each other.

Finally I understood why there'd be tears in my father's eyes when he raised an American flag. Witnessing the *Nimitz* homecoming, I felt such a surge of patriotism that I covered my heart with my hand and started to sing "God Bless America." A friend who was with me on that hilltop asked, "What's gotten into you?" Well, what had gotten into me was the idea for a series of five books. The first of these is titled *Navy Wife*. Keep in mind that I wrote them all in the late 1980s, before communication became as easy as it is today—before we knew about e-mail or cell phones.

Over the years I've often been asked when my "Navy" books will be published again. I'm very excited that they're coming out now. When you read them, I hope you'll appreciate the men and women in our military who've dedicated themselves to our national defense. I hope you feel the same as I did that bright summer's afternoon when I first laid eyes on the *Nimitz*.

God bless America and the United States Navy.

Sincerely,

Debbie Macomber

P.S. I love hearing from my readers. You can write me at P.O. Box 1458, Port Orchard, WA 98366 or visit my Web site at www.debbiemacomber.com.

Chapter 1

After walking over to the window in her brother's empty apartment, Lindy Kyle paused and let her tired gaze rest on the view of downtown Seattle. Dusk was settling over the steel jungle, and giant shadows from the skyscrapers fell into the maze of concrete across the picturesque waterfront. In another mood Lindy would have been struck by the intricate beauty of what lay before her, but not now.

Seattle, as Steve had claimed, really was a lovely city. When she'd arrived, she'd been so preoccupied with trying to find the address of the apartment and the appropriate parking space for her Volkswagen Rabbit in the lot behind the building that she hadn't taken the time to notice anything around her.

Now she sighed at the panorama that lay before her. "I'm actually here," she said, mainly to hear herself speak. She'd come to expect a lot from one western city. She felt as an immigrant might have years ago, sailing into New York Harbor, seeking a new way of life and freedom from the shackles of the past. Lindy had been bound, too, in the chains of grief and unhappiness.

Dramatically she posed, pretending to be the Statue of Liberty, her right hand held high as if gripping a lighted torch, her left firmly clasping imaginary stone tablets. "Okay, Seattle, give me your tired, your poor, your huddled masses yearning to breathe free." Lindy sucked in a shaky breath and battled back tears. "Seattle, calm my fears. Clear my head." She dropped her arms and swallowed at the growing knot in her throat. "Heal my heart," she added in a broken whisper. "Please, heal my heart...."

Exhaling raggedly, she dropped her arm and admitted it was too much to expect—even from a place that had once been honored as the most livable city in the United States. Far too much to ask.

Suddenly exhausted, Lindy picked up her suitcase and headed down the narrow hallway toward the two bedrooms. She opened the first door and stood in the doorway examining the room. The closet, which was partly open, displayed an organized row of civilian clothes hanging inside, crisp and neat. A framed picture or two rested on the dresser, but Lindy didn't pay attention to those. This had to be the bedroom of Rush Callaghan, her brother's roommate. Currently both men were at sea serving six-month tours of duty. Steve was an officer aboard the submarine *Atlantis*, somewhere in the Pacific upholding God, country and the American flag. Lindy had no idea where Rush was and didn't particularly care. Men weren't exactly her favorite subject at the moment.

She closed the bedroom door and moved on to the next room. A dresser drawer hung open, mismatched socks draped over its edge. Bulky-knit sweaters were carelessly tossed on the ledge above the closet and shoes were heaped in a pile on the floor.

"Home, sweet home," Lindy said with a soft smile. She really was fond of her brother, and although he was nearly ten years older, her childhood had been marked with memories of his wit and warmth. She laid her suitcase across the unmade bed, opened it and reached for Steve's letter. "Come to Seattle," he'd written in his lazy, uneven scrawl. "Forget the past and make a new life for yourself." Steve had had firsthand experience with pain, Lindy knew, and she respected his judgment. He'd survived the emotional trauma of divorce and seemed to have come out of it with a new maturity.

"You'll know which bedroom is mine," Steve's

letter continued. "I can't remember the last time I changed the sheets so you might want to do that before you crash."

Crashing certainly sounded inviting, Lindy mused, sinking with a sigh onto the edge of the unmade bed.

Although she'd nearly memorized Steve's words, Lindy read completely through the letter once more. Clean sheets were in the hall closet, he explained, and she decided to tackle making the bed as soon as she'd unpacked her things. The washer and dryer were in a small laundry room off the kitchen, the letter went on to say.

When she finished reading, Lindy placed Steve's instructions on top of the dresser. She stripped off the sheets, carried the bedding into the laundry room and started the washing machine.

When the phone rang it caught her off guard, and she widened her eyes and placed her hand over her heart as shock waves washed over her.

It rang one more time before she decided to answer it.

"Hello?"

"Lindy, it's your mother."

"Oh, hi, Mom." Lindy smiled at her parents' habit of identifying themselves. She'd been able to recognize her own family's voices since she was a child.

"I take it you've arrived safely. Honey, you

should have phoned—your father and I've been worried.''

Lindy sighed. ''Mom, I just walked in the door not more than ten minutes ago. I was planning to phone after I fixed myself something to eat.''

''Did your car give you any problems?''

''None.''

''Good.'' Her mother sounded relieved.

''Everything's fine—just the way I said it would be,'' Lindy added.

''What about money?''

''Mom, I'm doing great.'' A slight exaggeration, but Lindy wasn't desperate—at least she wouldn't be if she found a job reasonably soon. The unemployment problem was one she hoped to correct first thing in the morning.

''I talked to your Uncle Henry in Kansas City and he said you should think about applying at Boeing...that airplane company. He claims they're always looking for someone with a degree in computer science.''

''I'll do that right away,'' Lindy answered in an effort to appease her mother.

''You'll let us know when you've found something?''

''Yes, Mom. I promise.''

''And don't be shy about asking for money. Your father and I—''

"Mom, please don't worry about me. I'm going to be just great."

Her mother expelled her breath in a long, anxious sigh. "I do worry about you, sweetie. You've been so terribly unhappy. I can't tell you how disappointed your father and I are in that young man of yours."

"Paul isn't mine anymore." Lindy's voice trembled a little, but she needed to say it out loud every now and then just to remind herself of the fact. For four years she'd linked all thoughts of her future with Paul; being without him felt as though a large part of herself was missing.

"I saw his mother the other day, and I'll have you know I took a great deal of pleasure in looking the other way," Grace Kyle continued, with more than a hint of righteous indignation.

"What happened between Paul and me isn't Mrs. Abram's fault."

"No. But she obviously didn't raise her son right—not if he could do something this underhanded and despicable to you."

"Mom, do you mind if we don't talk about Paul anymore? Ever?" Even the mention of his name brought with it a sharp pain, yet part of her was still hungering for news of him. Someday, Lindy vowed, she'd look back on these awful months and smile at the memory. Someday, maybe. But not now.

"Lindy, of course I won't talk about Paul if you

don't want me to. I was being insensitive—forgive me, sweetie.''

"It's all right, Mom."

A short, throbbing silence followed. "You'll keep in touch, won't you?"

"Yes," Lindy answered and nodded. "I promise."

After a few more minutes of filling her parents in on the news of her trip, Lindy replaced the receiver. The washing machine went into the spin cycle behind her, and she tossed a glance over her shoulder. That was the way her world felt lately, as if she were being put through a churning wash. The only question that remained to be answered was if she'd come out of this drip-dry and wrinkle free.

Rush Callaghan stood on the bridge of the USS *Mitchell*, a pair of binoculars gripped tightly in his hands. He paused to suck in a deep breath of tangy salt air and sighed his appreciation for the clear, clean scent of it. Being on the open seas stirred his blood back to life after three long months of shore duty. He relaxed, home at last, as the huge 1,092-foot-long aircraft carrier cut a wide path out of Puget Sound and into the dark green waters of the north Pacific. Rush was more than glad. He had recognized from the time he was a boy that his destiny lay on the swirling waters of the world's oceans. He'd been born on the sea and he'd known ever since that this was where he belonged, where he felt truly alive.

Rush had dedicated his life to the sea, and in turn she had become his mistress. She was often demanding and unreasonable, but Rush wouldn't have had it any other way. A gentle breeze carried with it a cool, soothing mist. The spray came at him like the gentle, caressing fingers of a woman riffling through his hair and pressing her body against his own. Rush grinned at the picturesque image, knowing his lover well. She was gently welcoming him back into her arms, but Rush wasn't easily fooled. His mistress was fickle. Another time, possibly soon, she would lash out at him and harshly slap his face with cold, biting wind and rain. Her icy fingers would sting him with outrage. It was little wonder, Rush thought, that he'd come to think of the sea as his lover, since she often played the role.

When the *Mitchell* had pulled out of the Bremerton shipyard eighteen hours earlier, Rush had left nothing to tie him to the shore. No wife, no sweetheart, nothing except a Seattle apartment where he stored his worldly goods. He wasn't looking to build any bridges that would link him to the mainland. He'd learned early in his career that a wife and family weren't meant for him. If the waters of the world were his mistress, then the navy would be his wife. There'd been a time when he'd hoped to divide his life, but no more.

A quick exchange of angry words followed by an outburst of disgust from his fellow officer, Jeff Dwyer, caught Rush's attention and he lowered his binoculars.

"Problems?" he asked when Jeff joined him on the bridge.

Jeff's mouth tightened and he nodded. "The captain's just ordered us back."

"What the hell?" Rush felt a hot surge of anger pulse through him. "Why?"

"There's something wrong with the catapults. Apparently maintenance doesn't have the necessary parts to repair the problem."

Rush swore under his breath. The catapults were used to launch the Hawkeyes, Intruders, Tomcats and other aircraft from the carrier runway. They were vital equipment for any assignment at sea.

Fortunately the squadrons flying in from two navy airfields on the West Coast—a hundred planes were scheduled to rendezvous with the *Mitchell*—had yet to arrive. As chief navigator it was Rush's job to guide the carrier through the waters; now it was up to him to head the *Mitchell* back to the shipyard.

"I've already sent out word to the airfields," Jeff informed him. "They've turned the planes back."

Frustration built up in Rush like a tidal wave. After three months shore duty and a mere eighteen hours at sea they had to bring the *Mitchell* home to port with her tail between her legs.

"How long?" Rush asked between clenched teeth.

"Maintenance doesn't have a figure yet, but if it's as bad as it looks, we could be sitting on our butts for at least a week."

Rush spat a four-letter word.

"My sentiments exactly," Jeff answered.

Rush let himself into the dark apartment and set his seabag just inside the door. The way things were working out he could be here awhile. The realization angered him every time he thought about it. He moved into the kitchen and set the six-pack of cold beer on the counter. He rarely indulged himself this way, but tonight he was in the mood to get good and drunk.

Not bothering to turn on any of the lights, Rush took one chilled aluminum can and carried it with him into the living room, pulling off the tab as he went. Standing in front of the wide picture window, he offered a silent toast to the glittering lights of the waterfront several blocks below. He took a large swig of beer. Tonight something cold and alcoholic suited his temperament.

He took another long drink, sat on the sofa and propped his feet on the coffee table. What he needed was a woman. One sexy as hell, with big breasts and wide hips to bury himself in—one who would relieve his angry frustration. Rush frowned. The crude thought wasn't like him. He rarely allowed his mind to indulge in such primitive fantasies. But tonight, after watching weeks of planning and months of hard work go down the drain, Rush wasn't in the mood for niceties.

Against his will, Rush remembered the look in his friend Jeff's eyes when he'd stepped off the gangplank. Jeff had been hurrying to get home to his wife, Susan. Rush didn't need much of an imagination to know what Jeff was doing about now—and it wasn't drinking cold beer in a dark living room. He allowed himself to grin. Jeff and Susan. Now that was one marriage Rush wouldn't have bet good money on. But Susan Dwyer had pleasantly surprised him. When Jeff had left Bremerton earlier in the week, there'd been no tears in her eyes, only smiles. She'd been a good wife to Jeff from the first. Susan wasn't a clinger or a complainer; the only bonds she'd wrapped around her husband had been in his heart.

Rush had seen subtle changes in his friend since his marriage. He'd been looking for major ones. Over the years Rush had witnessed the power a woman could wield over a sailor's life often enough to recognize the symptoms. But Susan Dwyer hadn't been like some of the others, and Rush had silently admired her—and envied Jeff. His friend had gotten damn lucky to find a woman like Susan. Luckier than Rush.... But then Rush had given up trying.

The sound of someone moving behind him jerked Rush into action and he vaulted off the sofa. The bathroom door closed and he heard the rush of running water. What the hell! Someone was in the apartment. It had to be Steve. He moved down the hallway, looked inside his roomate's bedroom and cocked his eyebrows in astonishment. A silk robe was draped across the end of the bed and the room was littered with female paraphernalia.

Rush released a slow, exasperated breath. He'd been afraid something like this might happen. Steve was still working his way through the pain of his divorce and it had left him vulnerable. Rush was all too familiar with the seductive wiles a woman could use to cloud a man's better judgment. And now it appeared that some schemer was taking advantage of his friend's generous nature, planting herself in their apartment. Apparently Steve was still susceptible to being tricked and used. Well, Rush wouldn't stand for it. A surge of anger at the thought of someone taking advantage of his friend's kind heart made him clench his fists.

He'd gladly handle this situation, he decided. He'd get rid of her, and if Steve asked for an explanation later, Rush had the perfect excuse. After all they had an agreement about this place and it didn't include inviting women to move in. His mouth tightened into a narrow line. From what little he could see, this one had made herself right at home. Well, no more.

With beer in hand, he leaned against the wall, crossed his legs and waited. Within a couple of minutes the bathroom door opened and the woman stepped out. Her dark eyes rounded before she let out a soft gasp.

Obviously startled half out of her wits, the woman's hand flew to her heart, gripping the lacy edge of her pajamas. "Who are you?"

Dear God, wouldn't you know it, Rush groaned inwardly. This wasn't just any woman, but one as sexy as the one he'd been fantasizing about, with nice, round breasts and long, inviting legs. One look and Rush could understand why his friend had set her up in this cozy arrangement. Lord knew she was tempting enough. Her sheer baby-doll pajamas revealed peekaboo nipples, firm hips and shapely legs. It took him a full second to realize her hair was dark and nothing like that of the blondes that usually appealed to his friend.

She continued to stare at him, eyes as round as golf balls, her hands pressed flat against the wall behind her. She opened her mouth and stammered, "Wh-what are you doing here?"

Other than the small gasp, Rush noted, she revealed no real fear. "Isn't that supposed to be my question?" he taunted, and his mouth twisted into a cool, appraising smile. She didn't make an effort to

cover herself, but perhaps she wasn't aware of how
the muted moonlight played over her pajamas, giving him tantalizing glimpses of her full breasts. Then
again, maybe she was.

"You must be Rush."

"So Steve mentioned me?" That surprised him.

"Yes...of course." The woman worked her way
past him and retrieved her robe from the foot of the
bed, quickly donning it. She made an effort to disguise her uneasiness, but Rush noted that she was
trembling. Even from where he was standing he
could see that her heart was pounding like a jack-
hammer. She glanced his way once, silently appealing to him with those huge brown eyes of hers, but
Rush was unmoved. If she thought to practice her
charms on him, then she could think again. Steve
Kyle was his friend and he wasn't about to let his
buddy be used by this woman or anyone else.

As nonchalantly as possible Rush followed her
into the bedroom, ignoring the soft scent of jasmine.
"How long have you been here?" Her clothes hung
in the closet and her things were lined atop the
dresser. He lifted the sleeve of a blouse and let the
smooth feel of silk run through his fingers. From the
look of things, she'd settled right in as though she
owned the place. Perhaps she assumed she did; but
she'd learn soon enough.

The woman didn't answer him right away. Instead, she moved out of the bedroom and into the

kitchen and turned on the lights. "Only a couple of days."

"You didn't waste any time, did you?"

She looked at him as though she hadn't understood his question. "No."

He snickered. "I thought not."

Her gaze left his and rested on the partially empty six-pack of beer. The sight of that seemed to make her all the more nervous and she rubbed the palms of her hands together as though to ward off an unexpected chill. "You've been drinking." Her words sounded like an accusation. The woman's judgmental attitude only served to amuse Rush. He had to give her credit, though; under like circumstances he didn't know if he could have exercised such an impudent spirit.

In response to her statement he reached for another beer. His mouth twisted into a sardonic smile. "Care to join me?" he asked, gesturing toward the four remaining cans.

"No thanks." She tightened the cinch on her robe and squared her shoulders.

"Somehow I didn't think you would." Rush tossed his empty can into the garbage and reached for another. More to irritate her than anything, he took a long, slow drink, letting the cold liquid slide down his throat.

She watched him and braced her hands against

the back of the counter. "How long will you be...
staying?"

She had one hell of a nerve. "I think I should be
the one asking questions, don't you?"

"I—I suppose."

She continued to stare at him with those wide,
appealing eyes, and Rush struggled to ignore the
false innocence of her silent entreaty.

"I take it Steve didn't let you know I was coming."

"No, he forgot to mention you." It was apparent
to Rush that his roommate probably had no intention
of letting him know. It would have been easy
enough to let the matter slide since Steve would be
returning from sea duty before Rush was due back
into port.

"I'm Lindy."

He didn't acknowledge her greeting.

As though to cover her embarrassment, she
opened the refrigerator and took out a carton of
milk.

Rush watched her actions carefully and noted that
the inside of the fridge was well stocked. The observation only served to irritate him more. Knowing
how generous Steve was, Rush didn't doubt that
he'd given her the money to get set up in the apartment.

Lindy poured herself a glass and replaced the

milk. "This does make things a bit awkward, doesn't it?"

Again Rush ignored her. Instead of answering her question he pulled out the chair opposite her and sat down, nursing his beer. As hard as he tried, he couldn't take his eyes off her. She was more than just pretty. Delicate, he decided, with a soft injured look about her. Damn, he fathomed better than he would have liked what must have led Steve to invite this woman to move in. In addition to the fragile beauty, she was soft and feminine—the kind of woman a lonely sailor imagines sleeping in his bed, waiting for him. Rush understood all too well, but he didn't like the idea of some woman using his friend. Not when Steve was ripe for pain.

She took a quick swallow of the cold milk, her soft, dark eyes hardly leaving his. Rush was growing more uncomfortable by the minute. He didn't want her here, didn't want her anywhere near this apartment. As far as he was concerned she was trouble with a capital *T*. She must have sensed this because he noticed her fingers tighten around the glass. Obviously she didn't plan to make this easy.

"It would help if we could reach some kind of agreement to share the place—at least until you leave again," she said, looking both embarrassed and uneasy.

His slow answering smile was as cool as Rush could manage. He wasn't about to let a woman sway

him out of doing what he must, unpleasant as the
task seemed. "Listen, honey," he said brusquely,
"the only one of us who's going to be leaving is
you. And the sooner the better. So pack your bags;
I want you gone before morning."

Chapter 2

So Rush Callaghan was kicking her out of the apartment, Lindy mused. Terrific. What else could go wrong? The answer to that was something she didn't want to find out. Oh Lord. She'd known Steve's invitation was too good to be true. Nothing was ever going to be right for her again—she'd been sabotaged by fate while still in her prime....

A quick calculation of her limited funds suggested that she could possibly last two weeks if she rented a cheap hotel room and ate sparingly. Two weeks and she'd be forced to return to Minneapolis a failure. The thought wasn't a comforting one. Her parents would gladly take her in, but their excessive concern right now was more suffocating than she could bear.

With deliberate calm Lindy drank the last of her milk, carried the glass to the sink and rinsed it out. All the while her thoughts were a churning mass of wary doubts.

She would leave, she decided, because Rush Callaghan had decreed that she must. But she could see no reason to hurry. Simply because he was an officer used to giving orders and having them followed didn't mean she had to jump at his every command.

"Did you hear me?" Rush asked, his narrowed gaze following her deliberate movements.

"I'll be out before morning," was the only answer she would give him, and she forced those words to come out as stiffly as starched sheets.

It gave Lindy fleeting satisfaction to witness the surprise in Rush's eyes. He stared at her almost as if he'd been looking forward to an argument, to sharpening his wits on hers. Apparently he'd thought she would stand up and issue some kind of challenge. Well, Lindy just wasn't in the mood to put up much of a fight. If he wanted her out, then fine, she'd pack her bags and leave.

Wordlessly she opened the dishwasher and set the glass inside. His eyes followed her suspiciously, apparently disliking her cool compliance. For the first time he looked unsettled, as though it was on the tip of his tongue to suggest that she could stay until morning. But if the thought crossed his mind, that was as far as it went. He said nothing. Lindy sup-

posed he was right. She could see no reason to pro-
long the inevitable. But damn it all, she'd never felt
so helpless and lost in her life. A condemned man
walking to the hangman's noose had as many op-
tions as she seemed to have at the moment.

Lindy turned and left the kitchen. She tried to
walk away proudly, but her shoulders sagged with
abject defeat. She heard the kitchen chair scrape
against the floor as Rush stood and followed her.

Standing in the doorway to her bedroom, Rush
glanced at his watch. Lindy pulled out her suitcase
from under the bed and looked in the direction of
her clock radio, noting the late hour.

As though it went against his better judgment,
Rush stuck his hand in his uniform pocket and murmured. "Listen, tomorrow morning is soon
enough."

"Not for me, it isn't."

"What do you mean?"

"Never mind," Lindy said with a righteous sigh.

"Lord, how like a woman," Rush murmured to
the ceiling, the words tight and controlled. "She
tosses a dart at me and then refuses to acknowledge
it. What she really wants me to know is that she
couldn't bear to be in the same room with me. Well,
honeybunch, the feeling is mutual!"

Some of Lindy's control slipped at his taunt, and
she angrily jerked a blouse off a hanger. "I don't
suppose you stopped to think that I didn't move in

here without an invitation. Steve invited me. I have his letter right here to prove it if you'd take the time to read—''

''Unfortunately Steve didn't clear this cozy little arrangement with me,'' he interrupted, ''and I have no intention of sharing this place with you or any other female.''

''You men think you're really something, don't you?'' Lindy cried, jerking yet another blouse from a hanger. ''You like being in control, dictating whatever you wish on nothing more than a whim.''

He looked surprised that she'd revealed any emotion. Good heavens, just what did he expect from her? Lindy didn't know, and at this point she simply didn't care. When she'd finished emptying her closet, she whirled around to face him.

''All along Steve's been telling me what a great friend you are, a terrific guy. You should meet him, Lindy. I know you'd like him,'' she said sarcastically, mimicking her brother's praise. She cast Rush a disparaging look. ''Some roommate you turned out to be. I'll tell you one thing, mister...''

''Spare me, would you?''

''No.'' Lindy slammed the lid of her suitcase closed. ''You're all alike. Every last one of you is just like Paul.''

''Paul?''

Her index finger flew at his chest and she heaved

back in indignation. "Don't you dare mention his name to me. Ever!"

"Lady, you brought him up, I didn't!"

"That was a mistake. But then I seem to be making a lot of those lately."

"Your biggest one was moving in here."

"Tell me about it," she returned with a sneer. "Well, you needn't worry. I'll be out of your way in a few minutes." She yanked the suitcase off the bed and reached for her coat, preparing to leave. Boldly she paused and raised her eyes to meet his. With her lips curved upward, she regarded him with open disdain. "Steve is really going to be upset about this."

"I'll deal with him later." The look he was giving her said that if anyone had a right to be angry, it was him. As though Steve had been the one to let *him* down.

With a carefully manufactured calm, Lindy stopped at the front door, set down her suitcase and slipped the key to the apartment off her chain.

Rush held out his hand and she pressed it into his waiting palm. Once again he looked as if he wanted to say that she could stay until morning. She didn't know what stopped him—probably his pride. Men had to have their pride. No doubt he was aware that she'd take delight in throwing the invitation back in his face.

Lindy watched as Rush's dark eyes narrowed,

then she sadly shook her head. For years she'd been hearing Rush's name exalted. According to Steve, Rush Callaghan was both an officer and a gentleman. In the space of fifteen minutes, Lindy had quickly discovered he was neither.

"Bad judgment must run in the family," she said, more for her own ears than his. "If Steve thinks you're so wonderful, then my mistake about Paul seems like a minor miscalculation of character." With that she picked up her lone suitcase and pulled open the front door.

Rush's hand reached out and gripped her shoulder, stopping her. "Family? What exactly do you mean by that?"

"Steve Kyle, my brother. You know, the man who pays half the rent for this place? The one who wrote and claimed I was welcome to live here until I found a job?"

His fingers closed painfully over her shoulder and his eyes simmered with impatient anger. "Why the hell didn't you say you were Steve's sister?" He reached for her suitcase, stripped it from her hands and jerked her back inside the apartment. Rush slammed the door shut after her and studied her as though seeing her for the first time.

"Don't tell me you didn't know!" she shouted back. "Just who the hell did you think I was?" The answer to that was all too obvious and a heated flash of bright color invaded her neck and cheeks. "Oh, honestly, that's...disgusting."

Rush raked his fingers through his hair in an agitated movement and walked a few steps past her before turning around to confront her once more. "Listen, I didn't know. Honest."

"Does this mean I'm welcome to spend the night in my own brother's apartment?"

He let that taunt pass. "Yes, of course."

"How generous of you."

Rush picked up the suitcase and carried it back into Steve's bedroom, his jerky movements revealing both his chagrin and his anger. Lindy followed him, no longer sure what to make of this man. She knew Steve's invitation had been a spur of the moment thing. The two men easily could have gotten their wires crossed. From experience Lindy knew how letters could get held up in the military, and it was likely that Rush hadn't known she was planning on moving in. Still that didn't excuse his arrogant attitude toward her.

Lindy was two steps behind the man who Steve claimed was his best friend. Rush set the suitcase back on top of the mattress and hesitated before turning around to face her once more.

"I apologize. Okay?"

She answered him with an abrupt nod. His apology was followed by a short, uneasy silence. Lindy didn't know what to say. After a tense moment, she murmured. "I think the entire incident is best forgotten."

"Good." Rush buried his hands in his pockets, looking as uncomfortable as Lindy felt. "Of course you're welcome to stay in the apartment as long as you like. I'm hoping to be out of here by the end of the week."

"I thought you'd already left. I mean..."

Apparently he knew what she meant. "I had, but there were some mechanical difficulties and the *Mitchell* is back in the shipyard for repairs."

"For a week?" After nearly drowning in love and concern from her parents, Lindy had been looking forward to living alone. Well, so much for that—at least for now.

"Possibly longer, but don't worry about it. You're welcome to stay," Rush murmured, still looking uncomfortable.

Lindy guessed that he didn't often make apologies. "Thanks, but I have no intention of burdening you any longer than necessary. As soon as I've found a job, I'll be on my way."

"'Night," Rush said abruptly, taking a step in retreat.

"Good night," Lindy returned with a weak, dispirited smile.

Rush walked out of the room and Lindy closed it in his wake and leaned against the frame. Her mind was whirling. She knew even before she climbed

between the sheets that she wasn't likely to sleep
any time soon. Rest, like contentment, had been a
fleeting commodity these past few weeks.

Rush smelled fresh coffee when he woke the next
morning. With some reluctance, he climbed out of
bed and dressed. He'd made a heel of himself and
he wasn't eager to face Steve's sister with his head
throbbing and his mouth tasting like something
floating in a skid-row gutter. After he'd left Lindy
the night before, he'd tried to sleep, given up an
hour later and gone back to drink the rest of the six-
pack of beer and watch television. Now he was suf-
fering the consequences of his folly.

He sat for a moment on the edge of his bed, his
head in his hands. For years he'd heard stories about
his friend's younger sister. How intelligent she was,
how clever, how pretty. Steve was more than fond
of his sister. He adored her and now Rush had gone
and insulted her, and in the process maligned his
best friend. He should have realized that Steve
wasn't fool enough to set a woman up in their apartment. Hell, Steve was still so much in love with his
ex-wife that he couldn't see straight.

Damn it all, Rush mused, irritated with himself.
He shouldn't have downed those first two beers. If
his head had been clearer, he might have recognized
her name.

Rush frowned. He vaguely recalled Steve telling

him about some fancy job with a large insurance
company that was supposed to be waiting for Lindy
once she graduated from college. Come to think of
it, he thought Steve had said she was engaged to be
married this summer, as well. He wondered what she
was doing in Seattle, but after their poor beginning
he wasn't about to drill her about her job or problems with her fiancé.

Lindy sat at the kitchen table with the morning
newspaper spread out in front of her. She chose to
ignore Rush. As far as she was concerned the man
had all the sensitivity of a woman-hating Neander-
thal. Okay, so they were going to be sharing the
apartment for a while. A week, he'd said. She could
last that long if he could.

Rush walked over to the coffeepot, poured himself a cup, then muttered something that sounded
faintly like a growl. Lindy supposed that was his
own prehistoric version of ''good morning.'' She
responded in kind.

''What was that?'' he demanded.

''What?''

''That disgusting little noise you just made.''

''I was just wishing you a good morning.''

''I'll bet,'' he muttered, lifting the steaming mug
to his lips. He took a sip, then grimaced as if he'd
scalded his tongue. He paused to glare at Lindy as
though to blame her for his troubles.

Swallowing a chuckle, Lindy stood, deposited her coffee cup in the kitchen sink and left the table, taking the morning paper with her. It wasn't until she was in her bedroom that she realized she was smiling—something she hadn't felt like doing in a long while. Maybe having a man around to thwart and frustrate wasn't such a bad idea. With few exceptions, she'd recently come to view the opposite sex as both demanding and unreasonable. Rush Callaghan certainly fit the mold.

Gathering her clothes and a few personal items, Lindy headed for the bathroom. She'd discarded her robe and had just leaned over the tub to start her bathwater, when Rush strolled in.

"Are you planning to—" He stopped abruptly, his jaw slack.

Reluctantly Lindy straightened, gripping the front of her gaping pajama top with one hand. Color mounted in her cheeks like a red flag rising as she realized that her bent position over the tub had probably granted Rush a bird's-eye view of her rounded derriere. The flimsy baby-doll top no doubt gave him an equally revealing study of her breasts through the thin material. Incensed with herself as much as at Rush, she jerked a towel off the rack and wrapped it around her middle.

"Sorry," he muttered and quickly moved out of the room. He stood just across the threshold, watching her as though he couldn't jerk his gaze away.

He swallowed hard once before stiffly stepping away.

Lindy walked over and purposefully closed the door. To be on the safe side she locked it.

"Just how long are you planning to be in there?" Rush shouted, apparently not feeling the necessity to disguise his bad mood.

Lindy reached for her Timex. She looked at the watch and gave herself fifteen minutes. "I'll be out before eight." She expected an argument, but if Rush had any objection he didn't voice it.

Once Lindy was soaking in the hot bathwater, she found herself grinning once more. It was obvious that Rush Callaghan wasn't accustomed to having a woman around. The thought pleased her, but it didn't surprise her. The man was a grouch and dictatorial to boot, acting as though it were a woman's duty to humbly submit to his every command. There weren't many females who would be willing to put up with that kind of chauvinistic attitude. Lindy certainly wouldn't.

Nor had she been oblivious to his admiring appraisal. Just the memory of his slow, hungry look was enough to lift her mood considerably. After Paul, it did her ego a world of good to realize another man found her appealing. Plenty of doubts had surfaced over the past few weeks regarding her feminine charms, and it gave Lindy a cozy feeling deep down to realize she possessed enough allure to tempt a man.

Now that she had time to think about it, Lindy admitted that Rush wasn't so bad-looking himself in a fundamental sort of way. Until a woman recognized his condescending ways, Rush would undoubtedly fascinate her. He was well over six feet tall, with a muscled, whipcord leanness that spoke of discipline and control. His broad shoulders tapered to narrow hips and long legs. Without much effort, Lindy could picture him standing at attention in full-dress uniform, surveying all that was before him with an arrogant tilt of his square jaw. Lindy was surprised at the sudden strong charge of pleasure the thought gave her. Her mind conjured him standing tall and immovably proud, shoulders squared, gaze focused straight ahead. With the thought some of the pique she'd been feeling toward him vanished.

But what intrigued her most about Rush Callaghan, she decided, were his eyes. Although he hadn't said more than a handful of words to her this morning, his dark blue gaze was highly expressive and more than able to telegraph his sour mood. She'd gained a good deal of pleasure in provoking him and then watching his brows crowd his eyes, narrowing them into slits of cool, assessing color. Later when he'd confronted her in the bathroom, those same clear blue eyes had revealed much more.

As her mind continued to play with the thoughts, Lindy scooted down into the hot water, raised a washcloth and idly drizzled the water over her smooth, flat stomach.

In the hallway outside the bathroom door, Rush paced like a stalking, caged tiger. He'd checked his watch every damn minute for the past five. Just how long did it take a woman to bathe, for God's sake? Too damn long, for his tastes.

Finally accepting the fact that pacing wasn't going to hurry her any, he retreated into his bedroom and sat on the edge of the mattress. In an effort to be honest with himself Rush admitted that it wasn't the fact that Lindy was hogging the one facility in the apartment that irritated him so much. It was the tantalizing figure she'd presented to him when he'd inadvertently walked in on her.

Her firm young body had all but taken his breath away, and when he checked his hands he found he was still trembling with the effects of the brief encounter. He hadn't a clue as to why she would wear that silly piece of lace. The silky see-through fabric didn't hide a damn thing.

Like an innocent, he'd moved into the bathroom only to be confronted by the sweet curve of her buttocks and the milky white skin of her long, shapely legs. Rush could swear the woman's legs went all the way up to her neck.

If that sight hadn't been enough to hammer the breath from his lungs, having her turn around and confront him had. Her full pink breasts had darkened at the tips as she struggled to hold the front of her pajamas together. Not that her efforts had done much good. Her nipples had hardened and pointed straight at him as though begging to be kissed. Even now the image had the power to tighten his groin and make his breath come in harsh, uneven gulps.

A week. Oh Lord. He wondered if he could last that long. He inhaled deeply and closed his eyes. He hoped the *Mitchell* would be ready to sail by then because he didn't know how much longer he could contain himself around Lindy. He knew he had to avoid a relationship with her at all costs. In addition to being his best friend's sister, Lindy was hurting, Rush realized. Something had happened—he didn't know what, didn't need to know—but he'd recognized the heavy shadow of pain and grief that hung over her head like a dark thundercloud. Something had knocked her world off kilter. And Rush wasn't in a position to right it. He wasn't anyone's savior. In the meantime, the best thing that could happen was for him to keep his eyes and ears to himself and pray the *Mitchell* left ahead of schedule.

Lindy found Rush was in the kitchen when she returned from job hunting late that afternoon. Her day had gone amazingly well and she felt greatly encouraged. After filling out dozens of forms and passing a series of tests, she was scheduled for an interview at the Boeing Renton plant for the following Monday. The salary was more than she'd hoped for and the benefits substantial. She held high hopes for the interview. Perhaps the worm had finally turned and her luck was going to change. She certainly hoped so. But in the meantime she felt obligated to keep job hunting in case something else turned up between now and then. Besides she didn't relish lingering around the apartment, bumping into Rush everytime she turned around.

"Hi," Lindy greeted Rush cheerfully, draping the strap of her purse over the back of the kitchen chair. She was in the mood to be generous with her reluctant roommate. After her fruitful day of job hunting, she was actually beginning to feel a little like her old self.

It was obvious, however, from the vicious way Rush was scrubbing away at the dishes that his earlier dark mood hadn't improved.

He grumbled a reply, but didn't turn around. "Listen, I've got a schedule posted outside the bathroom so there won't be a recurrence of what happened this morning."

A schedule for the bathroom? He had to be joking! "Okay," she answered, having difficulty disguising her amusement. She opened the refrigerator and took out a cold can of soda, closed the door and momentarily leaned against it. It struck her then that she was hungry. She'd eaten lunch hours before, but with her limited funds she couldn't afford a fancy restaurant meal and had opted, instead, for a fast-food chicken salad. She had started to search through the cupboards when Rush turned around and nearly collided with her

"Excuse me," he said stiffly.

"No problem." She pressed herself against the counter as he moved past.

From the way he skirted around her, one would think she was a carrier of bubonic plague.

Without another word, Rush wiped his hands dry, rehung the dish towel and moved into the living room to turn on the television.

Since he didn't appear to be the least bit communicative, she wasn't about to ask him if he'd eaten or if he was hungry. Far be it from her to appear anxious to share a meal with Rush when he obviously wanted to ignore her. They weren't on a Sunday-school picnic here, they were merely polite strangers whose presence had been forced on each other.

Sorting through the cupboards, Lindy brought out spaghetti noodles and a bottle of spicy Italian sauce. After weeks of a skimpy appetite, it felt good to think about cooking something substantial.

The sausage was frying up nicely and the faint scent of fennel and sage wafted through the kitchen.

Lindy brought out an onion and had begun dicing it
to add to the meat when the knife slipped and neatly
sliced into her index finger.

The sight of blood squirting over the cutting
board shocked more than hurt her. She cried out in
a moment of panic and rushed to the sink, holding
her hand.

"Lindy, are you all right?"

She ignored the question. The cut hurt now.
Badly. Closing her eyes, she held her finger under
the running water.

"What happened?" Rush demanded, joining her
at the sink.

"Nothing." Already the stainless steel was
splashed with blotches of blood.

"You cut yourself!"

He sounded angry, as though she'd purposely injured herself in a futile attempt to gain his sympathy.
"Are you always this brilliant or is this show of
intelligence for my benefit?" she asked through
clenched teeth. He looked stunned for a minute as
though he didn't understand a word of what she was
saying. "Any idiot could see I've cut myself," she
cried, her voice raised and laced with a healthy dose
of fright.

"Let me take a look at it."

She shook her head forcefully, wishing he'd go
away so she could assess the damage herself. The
terrible stinging had been replaced by an aching

throb. She couldn't keep herself from bouncing, as if the action would lessen the pain.

"Give me your hand," he demanded, reaching for it.

"Stop shouting at me," she yelled, and jerked away from him. "As far as I'm concerned this is all your fault."

"My fault?" His expressive blue eyes widened.

"Any fool knows better than to keep sharp knives around." Lindy knew she wasn't making sense, but she couldn't seem to help herself.

"For God's sake, stop hopping around and let me get a good look at it."

Using his upper body, he trapped her against the counter. She really didn't have any choice but to let him examine the cut. Biting unmercifully into her bottom lip, she unfolded her fist, while gripping her wrist tightly with her free hand.

His touch was surprisingly gentle and she watched as his brow folded together in a tight frown of concern.

"It doesn't look like you're going to need stitches."

Lindy expelled a sigh of relief. With no health insurance, a simple call to the hospital emergency room would quickly deplete her limited funds. And although her parents were willing, Lindy didn't want to ask them for money.

"Here." With a tenderness she hadn't expected

from Rush, he reached for a clean towel and carefully wrapped it around her hand. "It looks like the
bleeding has stopped. Wait here and I'll get a ban-
dage."

It was all Lindy could do to nod. She felt incredibly silly now, placing the blame on him for having
a sharp knife. He left her and returned a couple of
minutes later with some gauze and tape.

"I didn't mean what I said about this being your
fault," she told him, raising her eyes to meet his.

His eyes widened momentarily, and then a smile
flickered in their blue depths. "I know," was all he
said.

Although she was willing to credit her loss of
blood with the stunning effect of his smile, there was
no discounting the way her heart and head reacted.
The simple action left Lindy warmed in its afterglow
long after her finger was bandaged.

Three days passed and Rush and Lindy became a
little more comfortable with each other. There were
still a few awkward moments, but Lindy discovered
that they could at least sit across the table from each
other and carry on a decent conversation without
risking an argument.

Rush tended to stay out of her way—and she,
his—but there were certain times of the day when
meeting was inevitable. In the mornings when they
were both hurrying to get ready to leave the apart-

ment, for instance. Twice Rush had gone out in the evening, leaving abruptly without a word. Lindy hadn't asked where he went and he didn't volunteer the information, but Lindy had the impression that he was simply avoiding being at close quarters with her.

Since it seemed silly for them to cook separate meals, they'd reached an agreement that Lindy would prepare the meals and Rush would do the dishes.

Rush was sitting in the living room when Lindy let herself into the apartment on Friday afternoon. She tossed her purse aside and slumped down on the opposite end of the sofa away from him.

"Any luck?" he asked in a conversational way, watching her.

Lindy noted that he looked tired and frustrated. "No, but I'm hoping everything will come together at the interview on Monday."

He stood, rammed his hands into his pockets and looked away from her, staring out the window. "I'm not exactly filled with good news myself."

"Oh?" She studied him closely, wondering at his strange mood.

"Without going into a lot of detail," he said, his voice tight, "the problem holding up the *Mitchell* isn't going to be easily fixed."

Lindy nodded and drew in a ragged breath, not sure what was coming next.

"It's going to take as long as a month to have the parts flown in," he continued.

"I see." She straightened and brushed aside a crease in her blue skirt, her fingers lingering over the material. "I suppose this means you want me to leave then, doesn't it?"

Chapter 3

"Leave?" Rush echoed, looking both surprised and angry.

Lindy bounded to her feet, her hands clenched at her sides in tight fists. "It's a perfectly logical question, so don't snap at me."

"I'm not snapping."

"A turtle couldn't do it better."

"Are you always this prickly or is it something about me?" He was glaring at her, demanding a response, the look in his eyes hot enough to boil water.

Although his voice was deliberately expressionless and quiet, Lindy knew by the tight set of his jaw that he was getting madder by the minute. Not

that she cared. The man drove her absolutely loony.
She'd never known anyone who could control his
emotions the way Rush did. Oh sure, he laughed, he
smiled, he talked, he argued, but in the entire four
days that she'd been living in the apartment with
him, he'd revealed as much sentiment as a wooden
Indian. Even when she'd cut her finger and hopped
around the kitchen like a crazed kangaroo, he'd been
as calm and collected as though he handled hurting,
frightened women every day of his life. Nothing
seemed to faze Rush. Nothing.

"Well, you needn't worry. I'll go," she announced with a proud tilt of her chin. "It won't be
necessary for you to ask twice." She bent down and
reached for the strap of her purse, her heart pounding like a charging locomotive. Moving was something she should have done the minute she realized
she wasn't going to have the apartment to herself.

"Damn it, Lindy. I didn't say you had to leave."

She blinked. "You didn't?"

"No. You jumped to conclusions."

"Oh." Now she felt like a bloody idiot. It was
on the tip of her tongue to apologize. She'd had a
rough day; the heel had broken off her shoe and the
job she'd gone to apply for wasn't the least bit as it
had been advertised. Although they'd offered it to
her, she'd decided against it. Good grief. She
wouldn't have been anything more than a glorified
desk clerk. Maybe she shouldn't be so particular, but

after four years of college she wanted so much more than to file papers and answer a telephone.

Maybe she was feeling a little guilty because she'd told Rush she hadn't had any luck when she'd actually gotten a job offer. And refused it.

They stood not more than five feet apart and his piercing gaze locked with hers, burning straight through her proud resolve.

When Lindy spoke her voice was husky with emotion, and her heart began a heavy muted pounding against her rib cage. "I lied."

Rush's eyes clouded, then hardened, and Lindy felt the dread crowd its way into her throat. Rush wasn't the type of man who would take something like this lightly.

"What did you lie about?"

"I got offered a job today. I turned it down." With her long tapered nails biting into the flesh of her palms, she explained the circumstances. "I thought you should know because...well, because I plan to rent my own place as soon as I can after I find something. But it looks like I could be around awhile."

A smile flickered over his lips and he appeared to relax a little. "I can stand it if you can."

"That's debatable."

They were both grinning then, and Lindy felt the uneasy tension seep from her limbs. Now that she'd explained things to Rush she felt much better. In

fact, possibly for the first time, she was completely
at ease with him. It wasn't that he intimidated her
so much as he challenged her. She felt as if she had
to be constantly on her guard with him. Watch her
step, keep the peace—that sort of thing.

"You must be hungry." she said, turning toward
the kitchen. "I'll get dinner going."

"Lindy."

She twisted around, her eyes questioning.

"Since it's Friday and we've both had a trying
week, how about going out for a pizza?"

The minute Rush issued the invitation, he was
convinced he'd done the wrong thing. His biggest
concern was that he was giving Lindy the wrong
impression. When the repairs on the *Mitchell* were
finished he'd be leaving, and he didn't want to give
his best friend's sister the idea that there could ever
be anything romantic between them. The circumstances in which they were living were tempting
enough, and here he was adding to the tension by
deepening the relationship to something beyond
their polite but strained friendship.

Hell, he wasn't even sure why he'd suggested
they go out. The last couple of nights he'd purposely
left the apartment and sat in a bar on the waterfront,
nursing a drink or two. The best way to deal with
this awkward situation, he'd decided, was to stay
away from Lindy as much as possible. Remove him-

self from temptation, so to speak. Because, damn it all, Lindy Kyle was one hell of a tempting morsel. Her young, firm body was ripe and it had been too long since he'd had a woman. Every time he was in the same room with her, he felt the charge of electricity arc between them. Until today, he'd been able to deal with it, and now he was purposely exposing them to God only knew what.

He wanted to be angry with her—needed it to dilute the effect she had on him. When she'd admitted she'd lied, he'd felt a reassuring irritation surging up inside him, rough and heated. As far as he was concerned, women weren't exactly known for their integrity. Although disappointed in her, he'd made a conscious effort to control his ire, knowing it wouldn't do any good to blow up at her.

And then she'd told him about turning down the job, her clear brown eyes soft and filled with contrition for having misled him. Her eager, young face had been as readable as a first-grade primer. She'd stood before him, so forthright and honest, and he'd felt something deep and fundamental move inside him. Before he'd even known what was happening, he'd offered to take her to dinner.

It was more than that, too. Steve's letter had finally caught up with him, explaining what had happened to Lindy. The poor kid had been through a lot. Apparently she'd been deeply in love with this Paul Abrams, and she'd been crushed when he'd broken the engagement. Rush had been crippled by emotional pain once himself. He knew from personal experience how devastating letting go of a loved one could be.

After reading his friend's long letter, Rush's opinion of Lindy had altered. Not that he'd made any dyed-in-the-wool assumptions about her before the letter's arrival. The fact was, he chose to think of her as little as possible. But after reading what Steve had written, he'd discovered that he admired Lindy for picking up the pieces of her life and forging ahead despite rejection and defeat.

Something else Steve had mentioned had strongly affected Rush. Throughout everything, Lindy hadn't shed a tear. Her entire family continued to worry about her because she was taking everything far too calmly, holding up much too well. It wasn't natural, Steve had claimed, sounding very much like the concerned older brother he was. Almost grudgingly, Rush found himself appreciating Lindy's courage and unsinkable pride. Not so long ago he'd been left to deal with the trauma of a lost love. He could still remember the pitying looks sent his way after Cheryl. The effort and control it had demanded on his part to pretend nothing was wrong, that losing Cheryl didn't really matter, had drained him. When all the while, every breath he drew had been a reminder that he'd been a fool to ever have trusted the woman. And worse, to have loved her.

Rush could identify with Lindy's attitude all too well. He would have walked over hot coals before he'd show his pain to anyone, friend or foe. Apparently she felt the same way. Maybe that was the reason he found himself wanting to spend more time with her, looking for a way to be her friend.

A Michael Jackson song blared loudly from the pizza parlor's jukebox and, much to her surprise, Lindy found herself tapping her foot to the music and wanting to snap her fingers. Rush sat across the booth from her, looking more relaxed and at ease than she could ever remember seeing him. A tall, frosty pitcher of beer rested in the middle of the table.

Lindy had already downed two thick mugs of ale and was feeling the dizzying, warm effects of the alcohol. Rarely had she tasted better pizza, and she'd pigged down three enormous slices, astonishing them both. Now she felt content and happy, two states of mind that had been sadly lacking in her life recently.

"If there was a big enough floor space, I'd want to dance," she told Rush, who instantly looked relieved—no doubt because he'd chosen a restaurant without one. Lindy giggled.

"What's so funny?"

"You!"

"I'm glad you find me so amusing."

"Don't take it personally. It's just that it feels so good to sit back and relax like this."

"That amuses you?"

"Yes, because you look like you've just been granted a pardon from the governor because you don't have to dance. And something else."

His dark brows shot up. "There's more?"

"Oh yes. For the first time since we met, I don't feel I have to keep my wits sharpened around you." She said it with a smile, hoping her good mood would cut any sting from her words. "In case you didn't know it, Rush Callaghan, you can be one hell of an arrogant jerk. Imagine posting a schedule to use the bathroom!"

His eyes narrowed, his jaw clenched in mock consternation, and still he looked every inch the sturdy, capable naval officer she knew him to be.

"There are a few truths about yourself I could enlighten you with as well, Lindy Kyle."

"Perhaps," she conceded.

He was teasing her and Lindy found herself warming to him. When he chose to, Rush could freeze out an Eskimo with one piercing glare. She hated to think of the men on the *Mitchell* facing his wrath because, although she hadn't seen it in full force, she'd witnessed enough to know his anger would be formidable. Discovering this gentler, fun-loving side of his nature had been an unexpected surprise.

Still smiling, Rush stood and threw a couple of dollars onto the table. "Come on, let's get out of here before someone pushes aside a few tables and starts up a band."

Lindy laughed and reached for her sweater and purse. Rush's hand lightly touched the small of her back as he guided her out of the restaurant. "So you really aren't going to take me dancing?" she asked, once they were outside in the cool June air.

"Not on your life."

Lindy released a slow, expressive sigh and glanced up into the dark, warmth of his gaze. A small taste of excitement filled her, and some of the heavy feeling that had weighted her heart for so many interminable weeks lifted.

"Would the lady consider a walk instead?" Rush said, his voice oddly tender, indulgent. He lifted his hand and rested it against her shoulder, his touch amazingly light.

Lindy had the impression that he'd rather not have his hand where it was, but that he couldn't help himself, and she waded through a surge of elation. It was marvelous to feel like a woman again, and she was highly aware of her power, however fleeting.

They strolled toward the busy Seattle waterfront, weaving in and out of the crowds that lingered on the sidewalk. The air was clean and fresh, smelling of tangy salt and seaweed, and although the sun had set, the gentle breeze carried with it a pleasing warmth.

Rush bought them coffee from a seafood bar and they silently walked along the pier, staring at the lights from the ferryboat as it glided across the murky green waters of Puget Sound.

"Can I see the *Mitchell* from here?" Lindy asked.

"No. It's in the shipyard in Bremerton, which is all the way across the Sound."

"You really love the sea, don't you?"

Rush's fingers momentarily tightened their grip on her shoulder. "Yes, I do. Did Steve ever tell you I was born on a ferryboat?"

"No."

"I think my destiny was cast then. My mother named me Rush because they were hurrying to get her to the hospital in time. Unfortunately, or fortunately, depending on how one chooses to look at it, I was born on the water."

"And have been at home there ever since," she added in a soft whisper.

He nodded and their eyes met in a brief exchange of rare understanding. Rush continued talking, telling her a little of his youth and his early days at Annapolis. He made a striking figure, leaning against the edge of the pier, Lindy noted. He paused and smiled down at her. His eyes narrowed briefly with appreciation and it was as if they had become two different people for this one special night.

Rush looked younger, Lindy mused, more open. For the first time since she'd arrived in Seattle, she felt that she was beginning to appreciate this complex man. Maybe because he was really talking to her, sharing a small part of himself with her. There was no pretense between them tonight. Somehow Lindy realized how rare it was for Rush to expose this amiable, sensitive part of himself, to let down his guard and throw caution to the wind. She felt as though she'd been granted a rare gift, one that she would look back on years from now and treasure.

They left the pier a few minutes later, discarded their Styrofoam cups and continued strolling down the busy sidewalk until they reached Waterfront Park. Lindy braced her foot against the bottom stair, which led to an observation deck and a museum on the second level.

"It's a beautiful night," Rush commented, staring into the sky.

Lindy had the feeling he was about to suggest they head back to the apartment. She didn't want the evening to end. Everything was too perfect for them to leave so soon.

"Come on. I'll race you up the stairs," she called, letting the breeze carry her challenge. Not waiting to see if he was going to follow her, she grabbed for the railing and hurled herself up the concrete steps, taking two at a time.

The wind, which had recently picked up, whipped

her hair from her face as she made a mad dash up the stairway, doing her best to swallow her laughter.

"Lindy."

Rush's exasperated voice was directly behind her, and not wishing to be outdistanced, she lurched forward.

He beat her easily and was waiting for her, blocking her way when she breathlessly reached the top.

"You little fool."

Still panting and laughing, she tried to leap around him but almost lost her balance. A look of horror crowded his face as he reached out to grab her, but Lindy quickly darted in the opposite direction. Rush tried to block her there, as well, and she shrieked with the sheer joy of the moment and scooted sideways from him.

"Lindy, stop."

She dodged to her left and when he followed her, she darted to her right, then triumphantly stumbled past him, running to the railing, her eyes wild with joy.

"I won," she declared triumphantly, swinging around to face him.

Rush collapsed on the park bench, barely winded. "You cheated."

"Oh, honestly. Can't you admit it when a woman outsmarts you?"

"I'd admit it if it was true."

"My foot, you would." Lindy slumped down on

the bench beside him, her breath coming in uneven, shallow gasps. Good Lord, she was out of shape. She let her head fall back so her hair rushed away from her face, granting her a feeling of complete freedom.

Lindy exhaled, dragging the oxygen through her lungs. "Oh, Paul, I can't remember a night when I've had more fun." The instant the name slipped through her lips, Lindy tensed. "I meant...Rush."

The excitement that had galloped through her blood just seconds before felt like a deadweight pressing against her chest. For one crazy moment she was paralyzed. She had trouble breathing, trouble moving, trouble thinking. Scalding tears burned in her eyes, and the huge lump in her throat felt as if it were monumental.

Moisture rolled down the side of her face, burning her skin like acid, and she sucked in a trembling sob.

"Lindy, are you all right?"

Rush brushed away a tear and his finger felt incredibly warm against her icy cold cheek.

"Something must have gotten into my eye," she lied, turning away so he wouldn't be able to see the extent of her emotion.

"Here."

He pressed a white handkerchief into her numb fingers, and she made a quick job of wiping her face dry. "I think we should be heading back. Don't you?"

"Anything you say."

He sounded so concerned when it was the last thing she wanted. Suddenly Rush was the last person in the world she yearned to be with. Escape seemed of paramount importance. Somehow she found her way to her feet, although the cement seemed to buckle beneath her shoes. With some effort she managed to keep her balance and rush away from the bench.

It would have been too much to hope that Rush would let her go. But oddly enough he seemed to appreciate her mood, remaining silent as he matched his quick steps to hers. Side by side they started up the hill toward First Avenue.

The climb was steep and Lindy was winded by the time they'd gone only a few blocks.

"I'll get a taxi," Rush said.

"No. Don't, please." She wanted to walk—needed to wear herself out physically so she could collapse in her bed exhausted. It was the only way she could guarantee she would sleep. The simple act of putting one foot in front of the other, climbing up one street and then the next one, seemed to help her contain her emotions.

By the time they reached the apartment building, Lindy's lungs ached and her calf muscles violently protested the strenuous exercise. She waited impatiently while Rush unlocked the front door.

He held it open for her, and in that moment she detested him for the small display of manners. Paul had impeccable manners and look what he'd done to her. Look what he'd reduced her to.

Without even glancing in Rush's direction she paused just inside the living room and said, her voice weak and faltering, "Thank you for dinner."

He didn't answer her for what seemed an eternity, and she had the impression he was willing her to turn around and face him. But she knew she couldn't without dissolving into wretched emotion.

"Anytime, Lindy." His words were low and as smooth as velvet.

"Good night." The sooner she got away from Rush the better.

"'Night." Again his voice was so gentle, so tender.

She made it all the way to the bathroom door before her gaze blurred so badly with tears that she had to stop and wipe the moisture from her eyes. Drawing in several steadying breaths between clenched teeth gave her some relief. She'd be damned before she'd cry over Paul Abrams.

Damned. Damned. Damned.

Without being aware of how it happened, Lindy found that she had stopped and braced a shoulder against the wall, using it to keep her upright, needing its support. She pinched her nose with her thumb and index fingers, willing back the release of torrential tears.

"Lindy, you need to cry."

The words seemed to come from a far distance, echoing around her in a canyon of despair. She dropped her hand and looked up to find Rush standing beside her.

"No," she said forcefully. "I won't."

"Don't let him do this to you."

She tried to push Rush away, but her effort was puny and weak. "You don't know anything," she cried. "How could you?"

"I know what it is to hurt."

"Not like this." No one could ever hurt this much. No one.

"Listen to me," he said, and his hands gripped her shoulders. But even his fingers were gentle when she wanted them to be hard and punishing. "Cry. Let it out before the grief strangles you."

"No." Still she resisted, wildly shaking her head. "No. I hate him. I hate him."

"I know, honey. I know."

The dam broke then, and the tears that had been pent up inside her soul, shoved down and ignored for so long, bled from her eyes. A low, mewing sound slid from the back of her throat, nearly choking her. Sobs overtook her, huge, oxygen-robbing sobs that shook her shoulders and made her breast heave.

Rush didn't try to hold her and she was grateful because she couldn't have borne being restrained. Unable to remain upright, she braced her back against the wall and slumped to the floor. She gently rocked back and forth, weeping bitterly for the innocence she had lost, and wailing for the love she had given so freely to a man who didn't deserve it. She cried until there was nothing left inside her.

Lindy started to retch when her tears were spent, and she knew she was about to lose her dinner. Rush's hand under her elbow helped her to an upright position and into the bathroom. He stood behind her as she leaned over the toilet. She thought she felt his hand on her back, but she couldn't be sure.

When she was finished he handed her a damp washcloth. She held it to her face, letting the coolness soak away some of the terrible red heat. Her eyes burned like fire, her throat felt gritty and coarse, and her hands shook.

"Here." Rush handed her a glass of water.

She felt an abundance of shame at having allowed him to see her like this, and worse, that he should be the one to take care of her. She sank to the edge of the tub, afraid her shaky legs could no longer support her.

"You're going to be all right now," Rush told her confidently. "It's over."

She couldn't look at him but nodded because it seemed the right thing to do. Rush had no way of knowing what Paul had done to her. No way of knowing that the man she'd loved and planned to share her life with had married another woman while Lindy proudly wore his engagement ring. Rush Callaghan didn't know a damn whit about shattered dreams or the pain of a broken heart. He would never allow himself to be hurt this way.

"Come on," he said. "I'll take you into your room."

She stood with his help, and he tucked his arm around her waist as he led her into her darkened bedroom. Gently he brushed the wet strands of hair from her face and lowered her onto the mattress in a sitting position.

"I trust you don't need anyone to undress you."

"No, I'm fine."

"It's a damn good thing," he said, and there was more than a trace of a smile in his words.

He started to walk away from her but paused just before he reached the door, turning back to her. "You're a beautiful woman, Lindy Kyle, and someday there'll be a man who will love you the way you deserve to be loved."

Her mother had said almost those identical words to her. At the time, Lindy hadn't been ready to accept them; she wasn't sure she could now. All through college there'd only been Paul. Every thought of the future had been linked with him. Every dream. Every ambition. She felt as if fate had sent her tumbling into oblivion, uncaring what ill fortune befell her.

But it wasn't in her to argue with Rush. Instead she brought her feet up onto the bed and pressed her head against the feather pillow. Her eyes ached unmercifully and she closed them.

"Did you hear me?" Rush demanded softly.

She wanted to shake her head that she hadn't, but there wasn't enough spirit left in her to challenge him. "I'm too selfish to pine away for Paul Abrams," she said, her soft voice trembling. "I'm not willing to be miserable any more."

Her words seemed to please him. "You're one hell of a woman, Lindy, and don't you forget it."

"Right." She couldn't contain the sarcasm. Although she kept her eyes closed, Lindy knew it was a long time before Rush left the doorway. His presence all but filled the room. Only when he'd slipped away did she feel comfortable enough to relax and sleep.

Lindy woke around two, her throat dry and scratchy. Her temples throbbed, and her eyes were red and swollen. She didn't turn on any lights as she made her way into the kitchen, preferring the shield of darkness.

The drapes were open and the city lights flickered in the distance. Taking the cold glass of water and the aspirin with her, Lindy stood at the window and expelled her breath in a long sigh. She'd made such an idiot of herself in front of Rush. The thought of facing him in the morning was almost more than she could bear.

Fresh tears dampened her face at the memory of the humiliating way she'd sobbed and moaned and rocked with grief. She exhaled a quivering breath and brushed her cheeks free of moisture.

"It's over, Lindy, there's no need to cry anymore."

She whirled around to discover Rush sitting in the darkened room, watching her.

"I'll cry if I damn well please," she hissed.

"There's no need to now."

Lord, she hated it when men thought they were so wonderfully logical. Everything seemed to be so cut-and-dried for them.

"Who made you king of the universe?"

He chuckled at that.

"I don't find that the least bit amusing. I honestly want to know what makes you think you know so damn much about human nature that you can decree when enough tears have been shed?"

"I know."

Lindy slapped her hand against her side in an action meant to reveal her disgust. "So the big lieutenant commander has spoken.'' She whirled around and placed the water glass down with such force that the liquid sloshed over the sides.

''How could you possibly know about loving someone and then losing them? You can't imagine what it's like to have your heart ripped from your chest and be left with a gaping wound that refuses to heal.'' She was yelling at him now, but not because she was angry. The memory of the way she'd broken down in front of him was more than embarrassing. Heated words were her only defense.

Rush was out of the chair so fast that it shocked her. He loomed at her side like a dragon, his jaw as tight and contorted as she'd ever seen it.

''I know more than I ever cared to.'' Each word dripped with ice, his message clear.

They stood, their gazes locked in the moonlight, glaring at each other, refusing to look away. She saw his pain then, as raw and jagged as her own. His guard was down. He'd lowered it for her tonight when she'd spilled out her heart, leaving himself exposed and trapped in pain-filled memories.

''Rush,'' she whispered, ''I'm sorry. I didn't know.'' Slowly, she lifted her hand and touched his shoulder, wanting to offer him comfort the way he had helped her. ''I didn't know.''

He reached for her then, crushing her in his arms, burying his face in the curve of her neck. He didn't fill in the details. He didn't need to.

Chapter 4

Lindy slept on the davenport across from Rush, but the sweet luxury of oblivion escaped him. Even now, hours later, he couldn't forget the unself-conscious way she'd wrapped her arms around him and held him, her tears soaking through his shirt. Rush wasn't sure who she was crying for anymore: him or her. It didn't matter.

Her body felt unbelievably good against his own, and her warmth had chased away the arctic chill that had seemed to cut all the way through to the marrow of his bones. He didn't like to think about Cheryl and rarely did these days. But somehow being a wit-ness to Lindy's anguish had brought the memory of his own bobbing uncontrollably to the surface of his mind. Like a cork, the remembrance of his love and foolishness had refused to sink, and he'd been left to deal with the pain that had suddenly seemed as fresh and real as it had been eight years ago.

The memory of Cheryl had weighed on him like a steel cloak, tormenting his heart and mind. He'd loved her with a love that was pure and innocent. A love so rare that he never hoped to feel such deep, heart-wrenching emotion again. Leaving her to go to sea had been the most difficult thing he'd ever done. Every day of the tour he'd written to her, spilling out his heart. On payday he'd sent her every penny he could, living on a bare minimum himself because it was important to him that she have the things she needed.

When he'd reached home port, he couldn't get off the aircraft carrier fast enough. After six months at sea, he was dying to hold her again, dying to love her. But she hadn't been at the dock. Bitterly disappointed, the only thing Rush could reason was that she was ill. Well, he'd been partially right. Only her sickness was of the nine-month variety. From what he'd learned later, sweet innocent Cheryl had shacked up with another sailor a week after he'd left San Diego. She'd apparently hoped to pass the baby off as Rush's. Rush, however, hadn't needed a degree in math to calculate the dates.

It might have made things easier for him if they'd fought. He might have been able to release some of the bitter anguish he'd experienced over her infidelity. But instead he'd simply told her goodbye and walked away, the diamond engagement ring he'd intended to give her seeming to sear a hole through his palm.

In the weeks and months that followed, his mind played crazy tricks on him. He tried to convince himself the baby was his, although God knows it was impossible. He heard from a friend that Cheryl married some poor schmuck fresh out of officer training within a month after Rush had left her.

A couple of years later he'd run into her in a bar. Her big blue eyes had clouded with tears as she'd told him they'd let something good slip away. With a wedding band on her finger, she'd placed her hand high on his thigh and suggested they get together for old times' sake. Rush had thought he was going to vomit, she repulsed him so completely.

He never saw her again, never wanted to. Cheryl had taught him valuable lessons, ones destined to last a lifetime. She'd destroyed a part of him that could never be resurrected.

The first faint light of dawn seeped into the sky, extinguishing the stars one by one, and still Rush couldn't sleep. But the even meter of Lindy's breathing as she lay sleeping on the sofa was a soothing balm and gradually he felt the rigid tension leave his limbs.

They'd sat for hours, his arm around her, her head

nestled over his heart. Neither had spoken—or
wanted to. It was a time to remember. A time to
forget. When she'd fallen into an exhausted sleep,
he'd gently slipped free of her hold and lowered her
head onto the sofa.

She was going to be all right now.

So was he.

Lindy squinted as the sun flooded the living room
and seemed to rest, full force, on her face, disturbing
her deep sleep. Her neck ached, and it was then that
she realized that her only pillow had been the small
flat decorative one from the couch. She felt disoriented until the memory of what had happened between her and Rush gushed through her mind like
melting snow rushing down a mountainside during
a spring thaw. She groaned and covered her face
with her hands, embarrassed anew.

Slowly, almost against her will, she sat up and
opened her eyes. She felt empty inside, depleted.
Shaky.

A quick survey of the room told her Rush wasn't
anywhere in the immediate vicinity, and she sighed
with relief.

Coming to her feet, she brushed the mussed dark
hair away from her face and stumbled into the
kitchen. The coffee was made and a note propped
against the base of the machine. Lindy reached for
the slip of paper and blinked several times in an

effort to clear her vision. Rush had duty and wouldn't be home until late afternoon.

Thank God.

She wasn't up to confronting him. Not now, anyway. What could she possibly say to him after she'd stripped herself emotionally naked and exposed her soul? Lord, she didn't know, but she'd figure it out later. Right now she wanted a hot bath and some breakfast, in that order.

By five that afternoon, she'd washed windows, baked a fresh apple pie and scrubbed the shower. Occupying herself with a dozen domestic tasks until she was forced into the inevitable confrontation with Rush.

She was frying pork chops for dinner when she heard the front door open, and she tensed, instantly filled with dread.

An awkward silence ensued when he stepped into the kitchen. Since she wasn't sure how to begin, she glanced around nervously and offered him a falsely cheerful smile.

Rush was frowning and she watched as his gaze bounced around the apartment, growing darker and more irritated with each passing moment.

Despite her best efforts, Lindy felt completely unstrung, and still Rush just stood there, looking straight through her with those impassive blue eyes of his.

"I baked a pie." It was an absurd thing to say,

but Lindy was quickly losing a grip on her determination to be cheerful and pleasant.

"That's not what I smell."

Lindy saw him wrinkle up his nose a couple of times, sniffing. "What are you?" she asked, forcing a light laugh. "A bloodhound?"

Obstinately Rush refused to respond to her attempt at good humor. If anything, his face grew more marred by dark shadows and anger kindled in his eyes. "It smells like pine needles in here."

"Oh." Why, oh why, couldn't he play her game? He had to know how difficult all this was for her. "I scrubbed down the cupboards. I think I was supposed to dilute the cleaner more than I did."

Her back was braced against the counter, her fingers gripping the edge. She could feel a pulse come alive in her temple. She'd had all day to make up her mind what she was going to say to Rush, how she was going to act, but her conclusions had been vague and fearful. That was when she'd decided she wouldn't utter a word about what had happened, praying he wouldn't, either. She should have realized Rush wouldn't let her forget it.

"You've been busy."

She nodded eagerly. "Yeah, I decided to spruce up the place a bit."

Her efforts didn't appear to please him. Damn, but she wished he'd say or do something to help her. He had to know what she was going through.

"You said something about pork chops being your favorite dinner," she offered next, almost desperate. All the while, her eyes pleaded with him. She'd just found her footing with this man, and now she was floundering again, her feet slipping out from under her every which way she turned.

"That was thoughtful." Still he frowned, his brow crowding his eyes, darkening them all the more.

Lindy rushed to the stove and used a cooking fork to turn the sizzling meat. She dared not look at him, and when she spoke the words strangled her. "I wanted to thank you, I guess."

"For what?"

Obviously Rush wasn't going to exert the least bit of energy to help her. The stoic look of the wooden Indian was properly in place once more and she wanted to hate him for his ability to disguise his emotions so effortlessly.

"Lindy."

She ignored him, flipping the frying meat when it was totally unnecessary.

"Lindy, turn around and look at me."

She shook her head.

"Those pork chops are going to turn into rubber if you cook them much longer."

Forcefully she turned off the burner and slapped the cooking fork on the stove top. "I could hate you for this," she muttered between clenched teeth.

"Well don't, because it isn't any easier for me."

Her chest was heaving with indignation when she slowly turned so that they faced each other once more. Nothing about him said he was the least bit uncomfortable. They could have been discussing the weather for all the reaction Rush revealed.

"Well?" she demanded, not having a single clue as to what he was thinking. He wore the hard mask of disciplined self-control, and she longed to slap it from his face.

"I'm embarrassed, too," he admitted finally.

"You? Whatever for? I was the one who made a complete idiot of myself. I was the one who was wailing like a banshee." She whipped the hair from her face. "What could you possibly have to be embarrassed about?"

He looked as if he were going to answer her, but Lindy wasn't about to let him. An entire day of worry and frustration was banked against her fragile control.

"Why couldn't you have let it drop?" she continued. "Trust me, I was willing to forget the entire incident. But, oh no, Mister Know-It-All has to rub my nose in it."

The muscle in his clenched jaw leaped so hard his temple quivered, and a strange light flared in his eyes. "I didn't want any pretense between us."

Defiance and pride filled Lindy's breast and her long nails threatened to snap as she continued to grip the countertop behind her. "I don't, either," she whispered after a moment, willing now to release her resentment and accept the wisdom of his words.

"I'd like us to be friends."

She nodded, dropping her gaze to the freshly waxed kitchen floor. "Lord knows, I could use one."

He smiled at that, and when she glanced up she noted that his eyes had softened perceptibly.

"How did you know apple pie is my favorite?"

Relaxing, Lindy returned his smile. "A fine naval officer like you should know the answer to that. Apple pie has to rank right up there with hot dogs and the American flag."

They both laughed aloud then, but not because she'd been especially clever. The matter had been settled between them and they were on an even keel once more. They could be friends.

"Well, how do I look?" Lindy asked Rush Monday morning. She stood beside the kitchen table, where he sat reading the paper and drinking coffee. Her interview wasn't scheduled until noon, but she'd been dressed and ready since eight, pacing the living room. Lord, he swore she'd straightened the same stack of magazines ten times.

"You're going to do great."

"You didn't even look at me," she accused, her hands clenched together in front of her. She was a picture of efficiency in her dark blue business suit, white blouse and navy pumps. If it were up to him, he would hire her on the spot.

"You look wonderful," he said, meaning it. Too damn good for his own peace of mind, if the truth be known.

She checked her wristwatch and nibbled nervously on the corner of her bottom lip. "I think I'll leave now."

"Good idea." To be truthful, he'd be glad to have her out of the apartment. But not because she was making a nuisance of herself. Oh sure, her pacing was beginning to get on his nerves, but far more profound than that—Lindy was beginning to get to him. Bad.

She reached for her purse. "I'll see you later."

"Break a leg, kid."

"Thanks."

Her quick smile ate like a sweet-tasting acid all the way through him. He'd been a fool to think their nonrelationship would fall neatly back into place after Friday night. He'd been a first-class idiot to believe they could just be friends. Oh, they were that all right, but God knew he hungered for more. Much more.

Rush's breath escaped on a long, disgusted sigh as he pushed his coffee cup aside. Every time he looked at Lindy his body started to throb. It wasn't even funny. In fact it was downright embarrassing.

He leaned back in the chair and folded his arms over his chest, trying to reason matters out. Lindy was years younger than he. Ten, at least. And she'd been hurt, the pain much too fresh for her to trust her feelings. To further complicate the situation, she was Steve Kyle's little sister. Rush might be able to overlook the first stickler, but not the second or the third. Lindy was too vulnerable now, too susceptible. And Steve Kyle was much too good a friend to lose because Rush couldn't maintain his self-control.

Lord, he wished she'd get that damn job and move out of the apartment. And out of his life. Once she'd cleared out, maybe things would go back to normal and he could concentrate on matters that were important to him.

That wasn't true, Rush admitted even as he thought it. He liked having Lindy around, liked her being there when he came in after a frustrating day aboard the *Mitchell*. Liked talking to her in the evenings. That was the problem in a nutshell. He liked every damn thing there was about Lindy Kyle.

Rush was mature enough, disciplined enough, to ignore the physical attraction, although God knows it was difficult. A thousand times he'd cursed the memory of that morning when he had found her in the bathroom, and seen her all soft and feminine. His mental picture of the way her breasts had peeped out at him, firm and round and proud, had the power, even now, to eat a hole straight through his mind.

For his own sense of well-being he couldn't allow his thoughts to dwell on how good she'd felt in his arms, or how she'd fallen asleep with her head resting securely over his heart. Nor did he choose to think about how he'd sat and stroked her hair, drinking in her softness, marveling in her gentleness.

Lindy's allure, however, was much more profound than the physical. In the space of one week she'd managed to reach into his heart, dragging the emotion out of him like hidden scarves from the sleeves of a clown. Each one more colorful than the last. Each one a surprise. Lindy made him feel vulnerable, threatening him in ways he'd never expected to experience again.

He wanted to stay away from her, avoid her as he had in the beginning. But Lindy was like a magnetic field that drew everything to itself. He couldn't be anywhere near her and not want her. Physically. Emotionally. Every damn way there was to want a woman.

He stood then, determined not to think about her anymore. A cold shower was what he needed to wake him up to a few fundamental facts. He wasn't an inexperienced youth, unable to control himself. Rush had been around the block more times than he cared to count.

With a fresh set of clothes, he stepped into the bathroom and shut the door. He hesitated, closed his eyes and slumped against the side of the sink. Inhaling the faint flower scent of Lindy's perfume, he released a groan that came from deep within his chest. The fragrance wove its way around him like an early morning mist, tempting him, enticing him, reminding him of everything he swore he was going to forget.

With his jaw knotted so tight his teeth hurt, Rush reached for the shower dial and turned it on full force. Grimly he wondered how much cold water it would take to distract him from the ache in his groin.

"Rush." Lindy threw open the front door of the apartment. "I got the job." Filled with joyous excitement, she tossed her purse aside and whirled around the living room like a ballerina, her arms clenched tightly over her breasts.

She was so dizzy she nearly stumbled, but she didn't care. Breathless and laughing, she stopped and braced her hand along the back of the sofa. "Oh, come on, Rush, you've got to be home!"

A quick check of the rooms told her he wasn't. The minute she'd been free, Lindy had hurried out of the Boeing offices, dying to tell Rush that the job was hers. The money was great. More than great. Wonderful. Health insurance, paid vacations, sick leave. And ten days off at Christmas. The whole nine yards—or was that ten? She didn't know. What she did know was that this wonderful, fabulous job was hers.

She couldn't have asked for a better position. The woman who would be her supervisor had taken Lindy around to meet her co-workers and everyone had been so nice, so friendly. Lindy had known almost immediately that she was going to fit right in.

"Rush," she called out again, in case she'd missed him somehow.

His name fell emptily into the silence. Oh well, he'd hear her good news soon enough. She went into her bedroom and changed into jeans and a soft pink ten-button Henley shirt, pushing the three-quarter length sleeves up past her elbows. She reached for her purse and as an afterthought scribbled Rush a note that said she was going out to buy thick T-bones, and when she got back they would celebrate.

By the time Lindy returned from the Pike Place Market, Rush was on the lanai and the barbecue was smoking.

"Hi," she called out, and set the grocery bag on the counter. "I got the job."

"I didn't doubt for a minute that you would."

Rush looked wonderfully relaxed in casual slacks and a light blue sweater that set off the color of his eyes to a clear cornflower blue. The sun glinted through his dark hair, and when he turned to smile at her, his face fairly danced with happy mischief, as if he'd known all along she'd do well and was as pleased as she that she had gotten the job. And exceedingly proud.

"Well, you might have shared some of that confidence with me," Lindy told him with mock disgust. "In case you didn't notice, I was a wreck this morning. Imagine leaving two hours before an interview." She could chide herself about it now, but she'd felt as if an army of red ants had decided to use her stomach as a place to dig their farm.

"I was confident enough to buy a bottle of champagne to celebrate," he informed her, moving into the kitchen and opening the fridge. He brought out the bottle and set it on the counter with all the ceremony and flair of a wine steward.

"Oh Rush, we can't drink this," she whispered, reverently examining the bottle. This wasn't the normal cheap champagne Lindy was used to drinking at Christmastime, but an expensive French variety, decorated with a gold seal and a fancy blue ribbon.

"Why not?" His brows shot up.

"It's too good.... I mean, I can't even pronounce the name of it." She tried, her tongue stumbling over the French vowels. In high school she'd taken a couple of years of the language, but she could never be considered fluent.

"You can't say champagne?" His voice dipped with sarcasm while tiny pinpricks of light shimmered in the depths of his eyes.

"Oh stop. You're being deliberately obtuse."

Already he'd peeled away the decorative top foil. "If anyone has reason to celebrate, it's you."

Lindy sighed and nodded, utterly content. "I can't tell you how pleased I am."

"You don't need to," he teased. "Anyone within a five-block radius could feel your happiness." His gaze held hers briefly before he dragged it away and started working to remove the cork.

Lindy felt strangely breathless and dizzy with joy. She was truly happy, when only a few weeks before she'd doubted that she'd ever experience elation or excitement again. Now she felt as though destiny had finally caught up with her again, and she was riding the crest of a wave, surging ahead, grabbing at every good thing that came her way. And lately, since she'd met Rush, there seemed to be so much to feel good about.

The sound of the cork popping and the bubbly liquid spraying into the sink caused Lindy to gasp, then giggle.

"Here, here," she cried, handing Rush one of the tall narrow glasses he'd set out. She didn't want any of this precious liquid to be wasted. God only knew how much Rush had paid for the bottle.

"A toast," Rush said, handing her a glass and taking his own. Tiny golden bubbles popped to the surface as if to add their own congratulations. "To Lindy Kyle, computer expert," Rush murmured, completely serious.

"I'm not really an expert."

"Are you always this argumentative, woman?"

"All right, all right," she laughed and licked the moisture from her fingertips. "IBM owes everything to me. Mr. Wang himself calls me his friend." Her eyes were laughing, her joy and enthusiasm exuding with every breath, because it was impossible to contain them.

"Mr. Wang?" Rush asked her. "What about Mr. Callaghan? Is he your friend?"

"Oh most assuredly. The very best kind there is."

"Good."

Lindy thought his voice sounded slightly husky, pleased, but before she had time to analyze it or study him further, Rush poised his glass next to hers. Gently they tapped the delicate rims together and Lindy tasted a sample. The smooth liquid was wonderfully light and mellow and so delicious that she closed her eyes to properly savor it.

"This is marvelous stuff," she said, taking another sip.

"I thought you'd like it."

"I bought us steaks," she said, suddenly remembering the sack. "And enough vegetables to open our own fifty-item salad bar."

Rush chuckled. "You get the salad together and I'll manage the steaks."

"That sounds like a workable plan."

"Good grief," he chided, unwrapping the thick

T-bones from the white butcher paper. "You're already using office lingo."

Lindy resisted the urge to swat his backside as he returned to the lanai, and turned her attention to the variety of fresh vegetables for the salad.

She finished before Rush did, and taking her champagne glass with her, joined him outside. It had rained for part of the week, but the sun was out this afternoon and the breeze was fresh and clean.

"The coals aren't quite hot enough yet," he told her, leaning against the wrought-iron railing, looking at ease with himself and his world.

Perhaps it was the champagne or the fact she'd stood too long in the sun. Lindy wasn't sure which to blame. But standing beside Rush she suddenly felt the overwhelming need to have him kiss her, the overpowering desire to glide her moist lips back and forth over his and taste the champagne on his tongue.

"Lindy?" He was frowning at her, and for a moment she was sure he'd read her thoughts. "What is it?"

"Nothing." She shook her head for emphasis, pushing down the impulse. It was insane, stupid, wrong. And yet something kept driving her. Something primitive and completely unmanageable. Before she could change her mind, she took both their wineglasses and set them aside, her hands shaking.

Rush watched her like a man in a trance.

She leaned forward and planted her hands on his shoulders, her intense gaze holding his.

At her touch, she felt a quiver work its way through his lean, hard body. He stiffened, his shoulders at attention as though a visiting admiral were passing by for inspection. But still he didn't try to stop her, didn't gently push her away as she thought he might. His hands bunched into tight fists at his sides.

Filled with purpose, and more determined than she had been about anything in a long time, Lindy stood on tiptoe and briefly touched her lips to his.

It was better than she'd thought, better than she'd dreamed. She cocked her head so their noses wouldn't present a barrier and kissed him again. Lightly. Tentatively. Shyly.

Rush stood stiff and motionless, but a low moan slipped from deep within his throat. His dark eyebrows cramped his piercing blue eyes, and he glared at her. If he hoped to intimidate her with a look, he failed. Lindy felt incredibly brave, ready to take on a fully armed armada if need be. Surely managing one weary sailor wouldn't be so difficult.

Rush closed his eyes then opened them, searching her face, his look tormented. He seemed to be telling Lindy to stop. Begging her to move away from him because he hadn't the will to move himself. But Lindy had no intention of following his silent demand. None. Instead she smiled boldly up at him, her heart in her eyes.

Rush claimed her lips then, and groaned anew as if holding her were the last thing in the world he wanted to do. His mouth clung to hers, warm and demanding as his tongue plundered the dark, sweet secret of her mouth, taking all that she offered.

His hands pulled her tight against him and he continued to kiss her again and again until she was flushed and trembling and her blood felt as if it could boil.

"Oh God, Lindy. No. No. This isn't right." His voice was tortured and barely audible. But still he didn't release her.

Chapter 5

Rush's face was hard. Harder than at any time Lindy could remember. His eyebrows were pulled down over his eyes, which were busily searching her face, seeking answers she couldn't give him.

Gently, his hands at her waist, he broke her hold on him and turned away, but not too far, because she was able to view his profile in the afternoon sunlight. He sucked in a giant breath and savagely jerked his fingers through his hair, his face dark and ravaged with what looked like guilt and regret.

"Rush," she whispered. "Listen...."

"No, you listen...."

The same mindless force that had driven her to kiss him led her now, and she moved behind him, wrapping her arms around his torso and fiercely hugging his back. She could feel the coiled resistance in him, but refused to release him.

"Lindy, damn it, you're not making this easy." His hands moved to break her hold and release himself from the trap of her arms.

At least Lindy thought that was his intent. But instead his fingers closed over her knuckles, squeezing her hands together with such force she nearly gasped with pain. But when his hand touched hers something seemed to snap inside him and he relaxed, causing her to melt all the more intimately against him.

She was shocked by how good Rush's body felt. He was tall and lean and hard and he stirred some inherent need in her.

An eternity passed before either moved. They hardly seemed to breathe. Lindy would have held onto Rush until the Second Coming if he hadn't broken free of her clasp and moved away from her. His breath was choppy then, as though it had cost him a great deal to leave her arms. His intense blue eyes stubbornly avoided hers.

"I think it would be best if we forget that ever happened," he said gruffly, and seemed to be engrossed in placing the steaks on the barbecue.

"I'm not going to forget it." Lindy didn't know why she felt she had to argue with him, but she did.

"I thought you were the one who was so keen on us being honest with each other."

"This is different." He shook enough salt over the meat to preserve it into the next generation. Pepper and garlic powder followed, so thick they practically obliterated the juicy T-bones.

"You said it was important there be no pretense between us," she pressed. "And you're right."

"Damn it, Lindy. Just what the hell do you want from me?" He remained hunched over the barbecue, refusing to meet her eyes. "Do you want me to tell you I find you attractive? Fine. You turn me on. I hope to hell you're satisfied now."

She couldn't have stopped the spontaneous smile that joyously sprang over her face had their lives depended on it. Just knowing Rush was attracted to her gave Lindy a giddy sense of power.

"I find you appealing, too," she admitted, having trouble keeping the elation out of her voice. Actually that was a gross understatement. She was drawn to Rush the way a thirsty flower is to rain.

"Well, you shouldn't, because..." he paused and forcefully exhaled a breath, looking both angry and confused.

Lindy's heart thudded expectantly. "Why not? Is it so wrong?"

Rush rose slowly to his feet then, faced her and placed his hands on her shoulders in a brotherly fashion, his eyes clear. Determined.

"Lindy, listen to me. You've been badly hurt recently. Devastated by a man you loved and trusted, and now everything seems to have turned around. You've got a reason to be happy, to celebrate. But my being here is much too convenient. It's only natural that you feel attracted to me, living at close quarters the way we do. You're a young, passionate woman, filled with the love of life and...you're excited now. I don't blame you, especially after everything you've been through. Your pride suffered a major setback not so long ago, and here I am like a savior, the means of salvaging it all."

"Rush...no."

"But Lindy," he continued, unwilling to let her cut him off, "you're too vulnerable right now. The attraction you feel toward me is only natural under the circumstances. But you've got to understand something important here. Given the same situation, you'd experience these identical emotions toward any healthy, red-blooded male. It's not really me who appeals to you, it's the thought of another close relationship."

"You can't honestly believe that. Why, that's ridiculous, Rush Callaghan."

"No, it isn't. Think about it, Lindy. Think hard. You want a man tonight." His voice was rough with intensity. "I can understand your feelings, sympathize with what's happened to you, but making love wouldn't be right. I'm not the one for this, and I refuse to take advantage of you. Find someone else to build your ego.''

"I find that insulting," she told him earnestly, but without anger. She had thought he might try to avoid her by starting an argument, and she refused to swallow the bait, no matter how much he irritated her.

"I'm not saying this to offend you. You're the one who insisted upon honesty. You got it." He returned to the steaks, as calmly as if they'd been discussing something as mundane as stock prices or the outcome of a baseball game.

"You're making this difficult," she said next.

"I plan to make it impossible."

"Honestly, Rush. Would you stop handling me with kid gloves? I'm a woman."

"Honey, that's one thing you won't find me arguing about." His words were followed by a harsh chuckle. "Now, come on. Be a good little girl and eat your steak."

The dishwasher was whirling softly in the background when Lindy reached for the telephone a couple of hours later. As soon as their meal had been completed, Rush had left her without so much as a word to tell her where he was going or when he intended to come back. The bloody coward!

"Hi, Mom," Lindy said when her mother picked up the receiver on the third ring.

"Lindy, sweetheart, is everything all right?"

"It's wonderful. I got a job with Boeing and start first thing in the morning."

"That's terrific."

Lindy could hear the relief in her mother's voice, and smiled, remembering again how great she'd felt when the personnel director had offered her the job.

"Sweetheart, I couldn't be more pleased. I knew everything would work out, given time."

"I have more good news."

"More?" her mother said, and laughed softly.

"I've met someone."

"You have?" The question was followed by a brief, strained silence. "Isn't this rather sudden?"

Lindy could all but hear the excitement drain out of Grace Kyle's voice to be replaced by weary doubt. "Now, before you say anything, let me tell you something about him. He's wonderful, Mom, really wonderful. He's helped me so much, I can't even begin to tell you everything he's done for me. He's a good, kind person. Honorable."

"Oh, Lindy," her mother said with a sigh, "do be careful."

"I will, Mom. I promise." The comedy of the situation struck her then, and she started to giggle.

"What's so funny?" Her mother obviously hadn't stopped to think things through.

"Mom, I'm twenty-two years old and when I told you that I'd met someone, you said I should be careful, like I was seven years old again and about to cross a busy street alone for the first time.''

"But, Lindy, you're hardly over—'' Grace paused and exhaled a disgusted, uneven breath. "I refuse to even mention his name.''

"Paul." Lindy said it for her. "He can't hurt me anymore. I refuse to let him.''

"That's nice, sweetheart. Now tell me—where did you meet this young man you think so highly of?''

Lindy gnawed on her lower lip. Explaining her living arrangements to her mother would surely be cause for concern, but Lindy wasn't in the habit of lying. "I met him a few days after I arrived in Seattle.''

"Oh. And what's his family like?''

"Mom, we've only known each other a little while. I haven't met his family.''

"But I think you should find out about them, don't you?''

"I suppose. In time. Listen, Mom, I just wanted to call and let you know that everything is going terrific. I've got a good job and I couldn't be happier. Really.''

"I'm so pleased for you.''

"I know. I feel good about everything, and I don't want you to worry about me anymore because nothing's going to hold me down again.''

"I knew you'd find your footing, given time.''

"I have, Mom."

"Goodbye, sweetheart."

"'Bye, Mom. Give my love to Dad."

"I will."

Lindy thought she heard a trace of tears in her mother's soft voice when she replaced the receiver. She was surprised to note there was a hint in her own.

With Rush gone, the apartment felt like an empty tomb and the evening dragged by. Lindy watched television for a while, worked a crossword puzzle and added an extra coat of pink polish to her nails. By eleven she was tired and ready to give up her vigil. Rush had been determined to get away from her, to leave her alone to recognize the foolishness of her actions. She knew what he was thinking as clearly as if he'd announced his intentions. Only it hadn't worked. If anything, Lindy was more determined than ever to get him to face the truth of what was happening between them.

Discouraged, she undressed and climbed between the cool sheets. But sleep wouldn't come. Instead all she could think about was how good it had felt to be in Rush's arms. How good and how remarkably right.

She recognized there was some validity to what he'd claimed. But he was wrong to think she was using him. The feelings she had for Rush had absolutely nothing to do with what had happened with

Paul. The attraction she felt for Rush was because
of who he was. She'd meant every word she'd said
to her mother. Rush Callaghan was an honorable
man, and there seemed to be few enough of them
left.

Rush had given her a priceless gift. Her freedom.
His patience and tenderness had released her from
the shackles of pain and remorse. He'd held her
hand and shown her the way out of the dark shadows. He'd led her gently into the warm healing glow
of a summer sun.

If he were with her now, discussing matters the
way he should be, Lindy knew exactly what he'd
say to her. He'd tell her she was grateful. She was,
but it was far more than gratitude she felt toward
Rush. He'd taken her wounded heart and breathed
new life into it. He'd let her feel again when her
every nerve ending had been numb, and her very
existence had seemed pointless.

She couldn't stop thinking about how perfect
she'd felt in his arms, her breasts flattened against
his broad chest, her nipples hard and erect. Just the
memory was enough to stir her senses back to life.
That brief time with Rush had produced an incred-
ible range of new awarenesses. His kiss had been
warm and tender, his lips lingering over hers as
though this moment and place were out of time and
meant for them alone.

His tender touch had brought with it the sweetest,

most terrible yearning to be loved by him. Completely. Totally. Lindy didn't need anyone to tell her that when Rush Callaghan gave his heart to a woman, she would be the most incredibly fortunate female alive.

Lindy had just begun to scratch the surface of his multifaceted personality. Over the years, Rush had built several thick protective layers around himself, and Lindy had only managed to peel away the top few, to gain a peek inside. But she believed with all her heart that underneath he was sensitive and strong, daring and bold, and yet in some ways almost shy.

In time, Rush would realize she knew her own mind—and her own heart. In no way was she rebounding from Paul. Her former fiancé had actually done her a big favor, although it had been difficult to recognize it at the time. Paul was weak. Blinded by her love, she hadn't seen it before. Paul didn't possess the principles Rush did, either. Rush, on the other hand, was noble, reliable and completely trustworthy. Lindy would stake her life on it. Her judgment had been poor once, but she'd learned something from Paul, and although the lesson had been bitterly painful, she'd been an apt student. She knew an honorable man when she saw one. And Rush Callaghan fit her definition to a T.

Still awake at midnight, Lindy bunched her pillow in half and rolled onto her stomach. She might as well climb out of bed and wait for him as toss and turn all night. She'd no sooner made the decision to get up when she heard the front door open.

Relieved, Lindy smiled and eagerly threw aside the blankets. She slipped her arms into the sleeves of her robe and headed out her bedroom door, impatient to talk to him.

Rush was just coming down the hallway.

"You're home," she greeted, not even trying to disguise her pleasure. It wasn't one of her most brilliant statements, but she didn't care.

He grumbled something that she couldn't make sense of.

"You didn't need to leave, you know."

"Yes, I did." He kept as far away from her as space would allow.

"Rush, we need to talk."

"Not now."

"Yes, now," she insisted.

"You have to go to work in the morning. Remember?" he argued, and rubbed his hand wearily over the back of his neck. "And for that matter so do I."

Lindy took a step toward him, and stopped. The cloying scents of cheap perfume and cigarette smoke clung to him like the stench of an infection. Shocked, Lindy tensed and braced herself against the wall to avoid getting any closer to him than necessary. She felt as though he'd driven a stake through her heart, so violent was the rush of pain. Rush had left her arms, scoffed at her timid efforts at lovemaking and gone to another. Someone with far more experience than she.

She glared at him through wide, angry eyes. "You're disgusting." She spat the words vengefully with all the vehemence her heart could muster. Then she whirled around and returned to her room, slamming the door with such force that the picture of her family on the dresser tumbled to the carpet.

Rush didn't bother to follow her and Lindy was glad.

She was trembling uncontrollably when she sank onto the edge of her mattress. The honorable man she'd been so willing to place on a pedestal possessed clay feet. Clay feet and a clay heart.

Lindy may have slept at some time during the long night that followed, but she doubted it. She was so furious she couldn't allow herself to relax enough to sleep. She had no hold on Rush, she realized. There was no commitment between them. A few kisses were all they'd ever shared, and yet she wanted to throttle him.

Apparently she wasn't as apt a student as she'd thought, and she didn't know which had disappointed her more—Rush's behavior or her own inability to judge men.

Rush heard Lindy tossing and turning in her room long after he'd retired to his own room. He knew

what she believed and had purposely let her go on
thinking it, hoping she'd forget this silly notion
about letting a romance develop between them. That
had been his original intention. But when he'd seen
the flash of pain in her eyes, he knew he couldn't
go through with it. Unfortunately Lindy wasn't in
any mood to carry on a levelheaded conversation,
he'd decided. He'd explain things in the morning.

Rush had gotten out of the apartment as soon as
he could following dinner, afraid of what might happen if he stayed. The truth of the matter was that it
had taken every damn bit of restraint he'd possessed
to walk away from Lindy. The cold beer he had
nursed in a sleazy waterfront bar was small com-
pensation for his considerable sacrifice.

His biggest problem was that he believed every
word he'd said to Lindy. She was vulnerable right
now. Vulnerable and trusting. A lethal combination
as far as Rush was concerned. If he loved her the
way she wanted, she'd wake in the morning filled
with regrets. Rush couldn't do that to her. Hell, if
he was honest, he couldn't do it to himself. He
wasn't so much a fool not to recognize that loving
Lindy once would never be enough. A sample would
only create the need for more. Much more.

The simple act of kissing and holding her had
nearly defeated him. When she'd leaned up and
brushed her lips over his, his body had fired to life

with a heat that had threatened to consume him. It had demanded every part of his considerable self-control not to lift her into his arms and carry her into his bedroom.

The sweet little witch must have known it, too. She'd pressed her softness against him, fully conscious of what the intimacy was doing to him. And then she'd paused and looked up at him, her eyes wide and trusting and filled with such delectable love that it was more than a mere man could resist. He'd kissed her until he'd felt her weak and trembling in his arms. He had no idea what had stopped him then, but whatever it was, he was grateful.

Escape had been his only alternative, and he'd left the apartment when he could. He didn't want to be in the bar, but after a brisk walk there hadn't been anyplace else he knew to go. A woman who often loitered there had strolled up to his table, sat down without an invitation and tried to start a conversation. Rush had glared at her and told her wasn't in the mood for company. Apparently she'd taken his words as a challenge and before he could stop her, her arms were all over him.

Rush didn't realize the scent of her sickeningly sweet perfume had stayed with him until he saw Lindy's look of complete disgust.

He was going to settle that matter first thing in the morning.

* * *

It was with a sense of righteousness that Lindy snapped a rock-music tape into her cassette player and turned it up full blast. Tapping her foot to the loud music, she wove the hot curling iron through her hair and waited. Within a couple of minutes, Rush staggered into the bathroom, apparently having just awakened, looking as if he intended to hurl her portable stereo out the living room window.

"Is that really necessary?" he shouted.

With deliberately slow movements Lindy turned down the volume. She regarded him with wide, innocent eyes. "What did you say?"

"Is that god-awful music necessary?"

It gave her a good deal of pleasure to smile sweetly back at him and ask, "Did I wake you? I'm so sorry, Rush."

"I'll bet," he grumbled and turned to stumble back to his room.

Lindy loved it.

Her sense of timing couldn't have been more perfect some time later when they met again in the kitchen. He grumbled something that sounded faintly like a plea for coffee. He had just gotten down a mug and started to pour himself a cup when she switched on the blender full blast. Hot coffee splattered over the counter and Rush jumped back, cursing savagely.

He whirled around to face her and once more Lindy gave him her brightest smile. She finished her task and asked, "Would you like some orange juice?"

"No," he grumbled.

She swallowed a laugh and with a good deal of ceremony, poured herself a glass.

Rush was studying her with a tight frown. "Now I know what they mean when they say 'hell hath no fury like a woman scorned.'"

Lindy gave him a vague look. "I'm sure I don't know what you mean."

"Like hell," he exploded. "Exactly how long is it going to take you to properly mete out justice?"

"Rush, I think you got out of the wrong side of bed this morning. You seem to be imagining all sorts of things. What could I possibly be angry about?" Already she was feeling better. Okay, so maybe her revenge was a tad childish, but Rush deserved everything he got—in triplicate.

"Damn it, Lindy. You've got the wrong idea here."

"Wrong idea about what?" She batted her thick lashes a couple of times for effect and had the satisfaction of seeing him clench his jaw. From experience Lindy knew mornings had never been Rush's favorite time of day. He looked disoriented, out of sorts and more than a little lost in knowing how to deal with her. As far as Lindy was concerned, Rush's confusion was poetic justice.

"While I'm still alive and breathing," he managed, "I think you'd better know there's been a minor misunderstanding here."

"I haven't the slightest idea what you're talking about," she returned, her look as earnest as she could make it and still hold back her amusement.

His hand slammed against the counter. "And I'm sure you know exactly what I'm talking about," he countered, unable to restrain his fury. "You've tried and convicted me without knowing the details."

The particulars were the last thing Lindy wanted to hear.

"Spare me, please," she told him, the amusement of her game vanishing. "You can sleep with a harem for all I care." It astonished her how easily the lie slipped from her lips. Rarely had she been more bitterly disappointed in anyone than she had been in Rush.

"Lindy..."

She cut him off with a quick shake of her head. "I wish I had more time to sort this out," she lied again, but not as smoothly this time. "But in case you've forgotten, I've got a job to go to."

She walked away from him and was already in the living room when she paused to add, "You were right about one thing, though. I'm not ready for another relationship." She turned to face him then. "You don't need to worry about trying to clear the air. I understand, Rush, far better than you know."

His eyes held hers and a strong current of energy

passed between them. As always she could read little in his impassive expression. But he must have agreed with her because he said nothing, and she hurriedly walked away, eager to escape.

It was while she was brushing her teeth that a sheen of tears brightened her eyes. After everything that had happened to her, it was a surprise. She'd assumed she had more control of her emotions than this; she blamed the tears on lack of sleep.

With her purse in her hand she headed for the front door. She'd learned several lessons in the past few months, but they didn't seem to be getting any easier.

Walking down the hallway, she was forced to pass Rush, who was sitting on the sofa in the living room. She forced a smile and squared her shoulders, prepared to move past him with her head high.

Just as she reached him, Rush's arm reached out, grabbed her hand and stopped her cold. His eyes held her more tightly than any vise.

"I won't have you face your first day on the job with doubts. There was no one last night, Lindy. No one but you."

She blinked back the surprise and uncertainty, not sure what to believe. The evidence had reeked from him.

Rush tugged at her arm, bringing her closer. When she was within easy reach, he wrapped his arm around her waist and brought her down onto his lap. She landed there with a plop. His hands found their way to her face and he turned her head so her unwilling gaze was forced to meet his.

"I can't let you go on thinking I could've touched another woman after kissing you." His eyes filled with an emotion so powerful that Lindy couldn't speak. Gone was the mask—lowered or destroyed, she didn't know which—and what she saw in his wonderful eyes gave flight to her heart. His look was innocent, youthful almost. Seeking. He needed her to believe him, was pleading with her in a way she knew was foreign to this proud man.

Tears pooled in her eyes, and she nodded, silently telling him that she trusted his word.

The pad of his thumb wiped the moisture from the high arch of her cheek.

"Damn it, Lindy. We're in one fine mess here," he said, his voice gruff with emotion. "I want you like hell. What are we going to do?" His warm mouth, only inches from hers, brushed lightly over her parted lips.

Lindy just managed to stifle a groan and kissed him back softly, her mouth lingering over his own, needing his warmth.

By this time he'd wrapped her in his embrace. As though they had all the time in the world, Rush brought her lips down to his own with an agonizing slowness. The kiss was filled with such aching tenderness, such sweet torment that the fresh tears rolled unheeded down the side of her face.

"I should have trusted you," she told him brokenly. "I should have known."

"Lindy...don't cry, please. It's all right. It doesn't matter." He pulled her more completely into his embrace and held her tightly.

The memory of his look when he'd stumbled into the bathroom caused her to laugh and cry at the same time.

"Honey...please. I can't bear the thought that I've made you cry. You are crying, aren't you?"

Lindy laughed aloud, then sobbed. She reached for his hand to kiss his knuckles. "Did you burn yourself when you spilled the coffee?"

He looked at her as though they should give serious consideration to having her committed to a mental facility. "No," he said tightly.

"I'm so sorry," she told him, spreading kisses over the edge of his jaw. "Oh, Rush, I thought horrible things of you. I thought—"

"I can guess," he muttered, cutting her off.

"But you're good and honorable and I was so wrong."

He chuckled and shook his head. "If you had a hint of what I was thinking of doing right now, you'd amend the honorable portion."

It was difficult to read his expression, but what she saw there caused her to wrap her arms around his neck and kiss him with a hunger that left them both shaking.

"Shall I tell you what I'm thinking, Rush Callaghan?"

Chapter 6

"Rush, guess what?" Breathless with excitement, Lindy let herself into the apartment and stopped abruptly, swallowing the remainder of her good news. Another man was standing next to Rush, and it looked as though the two had been arguing, or at least heatedly discussing something.

For the first time in recent memory, Rush didn't look pleased to see her. Apparently she'd arrived at the worst possible time. Her dark eyes met his and she offered a silent apology. His brief smile both reassured and warmed her.

After an awkward moment, Rush stepped forward. "Lindy, this is Jeff Dwyer. Jeff, this is Lindy Kyle, Steve Kyle's little sister."

Jeff resembled a fat cat who had just been presented with a pitcher of rich cream. The corners of
his mouth twitched with the effort to suppress a
smile, and his eyes fairly danced with mischief and
delight. "I can't tell you how pleased I am to meet
you, Lindy."

"Thank you." Her gaze moved from Rush to Jeff
and then back to Rush, who gave her a fleeting smile
that revealed his chagrin. He wasn't overly pleased
about something, but he wasn't angry, either.

"Since Rush didn't bother to explain, I will," Jeff
went on to say. "We're both officers aboard the
Mitchell. Rush and I've worked together for the past
four years." He hesitated and rubbed the side of his
jaw. "Until recently I thought I knew everything
there was about my fellow officer, but I guess I was
wrong."

Rush placed his hands in his pants pockets, ignoring the comment. "Jeff and his wife Susan are
visiting downtown Seattle this afternoon."

Jeff couldn't have looked more pleased. Lindy
didn't know what was happening between the two
men, but she'd apparently loused things up for Rush.

"Sue's having the twins' pictures taken at one of
those fancy studios," Jeff continued. "She didn't
seem to need me, so I thought I'd stop off and see
my good buddy Rush."

Lindy nodded, not knowing how else to respond.

"How long have you—ah, been living here?" Jeff asked.

Unsure, Lindy's gaze sought Rush's.

"It's not what you're implying, Jeff." Rush's frown was fierce as he glared at his friend. "In case you didn't hear me the first time, I'll say it once more. Lindy is Steve Kyle's little sister."

Again the edges of the other man's mouth moved spastically. Jeff looked to be exerting a good deal of effort to hold back his amusement. The more pleased the other man's look became, the darker Rush's frown grew.

"I heard you," Jeff said.

"Isn't it about time for you to pick up Susan and the kids?" Rush asked in an emotionless tone that was devoid of humor.

Jeff made a show of looking at his wristwatch. "I suppose," he admitted reluctantly. His gaze drifted to Lindy. "It was a pleasure to meet you. A real pleasure. Next time, I'll bring Sue along."

"I'd like that."

Rush was already standing next to the front door when Jeff left her. Lindy could vaguely hear the two exchange farewells followed by a couple of heated whispers.

"What was that all about?" she asked, once Rush had returned.

"Nothing."

"Don't give me that, Rush Callaghan. I know better."

He lapsed into silence for a moment. "Jeff came over to investigate a suspicion."

"Oh?"

"How did your day go?"

His effort to change the subject wasn't subtle, but Lindy could tell pressuring him to explain what had been going on between him and Jeff Dwyer wouldn't do her any good.

"Oh," she said, her eyes rounding with excitement. "I nearly forgot." Her hands eagerly started digging through her purse, tossing aside her compact and eel-skin wallet in her rush. Triumphantly she held up two tickets. "I got box seats for the Mariners' game tonight." When Rush just stood there staring at her, she blinked back her disappointment. She'd hoped he'd be as enthusiastic about attending the game as she was. "You do like baseball, don't you?"

His nod was decidedly absent. "Box seats?"

"On the one-hundred level. A girl I work with got them through the office. She can't go tonight, and asked if I could use them." Lindy had been so eager she could hardly make it back to the apartment fast enough, convinced Rush would want to see the Mariners play as much as she did. But looking at him now, she wasn't sure what to think. "Why are you looking at me like that?'' she demanded, a little piqued.

''Like what?''

''Like that.... Just now.''

He shrugged. ''I was just thinking about something Jeff said. I'm sorry. Did you say something I missed?''

Slowly Lindy shook her head. He hadn't told her any part of his conversation with his friend, and Lindy knew it would be useless to even try to get him to discuss the details with her.

''Do you want to go to the game or would you rather skip the whole thing?'' She tried to sound nonchalant, but she was really hoping Rush would want to attend the game.

''The game, of course. Don't you think you'd better change clothes? Starting time is in another forty-five minutes.''

''Right.'' Still confused, Lindy moved down the hallway to her bedroom. She didn't know what to make of Rush today. They'd been getting along so well lately, spending as much time together as possible, cramming all they could into the days and nights before the *Mitchell* left.

In three days they'd done something together every night. Tuesday he'd taken her to the Woodland Park Zoo, and they'd fed peanuts to the elephants and been splashed while watching the playful antics of the seals. Wednesday they'd gone on a picnic on the shores of Lake Washington, where Rush had lain on the sweet-scented lawn, resting his head on her thigh while he nibbled on a long blade of grass. Thursday they'd eaten fish and chips on the waterfront and strolled hand in hand in and out of the tourist shops that dotted the wharf. Each night they'd laughed and joked and talked freely. And each night Rush had kissed her. Once. And only once. As though anything more would be too much temptation for him to handle. Rush treated her with kid gloves, touching her as if he were handling live ammunition. His kiss was always gentle, always controlled—too controlled to suit Lindy. If she hadn't felt the soul-wrenching reluctance and regret in every part of him when he gently left her arms, she would have been deeply discouraged.

Lindy knew that Rush was having problems dealing with the emotions she aroused in him. He didn't trust their attraction. Didn't trust her, believing she couldn't possibly know her own heart so soon after Paul. And perhaps, Lindy realized, Rush didn't trust himself. He'd certainly gone out of his way to behave like an endearing older brother—except when he lowered his guard just a little each night to kiss her. He wanted her. He'd told her as much, and she wanted him. But the time for them wasn't right.

As fast as she could Lindy changed out of her work clothes and rejoined Rush in the kitchen, prepared to hurry to the baseball game. He took one look at her and burst out laughing.

"What's so funny?"

"You. I thought you said we were going to watch the game. You look like you plan to participate in it."

She'd chosen faded jeans, a Mariner T-shirt and Steve's old baseball cap. "Have you got a problem with this, fellow?" she asked him, her eyes sparkling with fun and laughter.

Still grinning, Rush shook his head. "Come on, Babe Ruth, we've got a game to see."

They were settled in their box seats with foot-long hot dogs, a bag of peanuts and cold drinks by the time the first pitch was tossed. Rush had never been much into baseball. Football was his game, but he couldn't have refused Lindy anything. Her energy and enthusiasm for life were like a breath of fresh tangy air after a storm at sea. Being with her stirred his senses to vibrant life and made him glad for who and what he was. There were odd moments, now and then, when he resisted the magnetic pull he felt toward her and recounted the arguments—that she was too young, too vulnerable and his best friend's sister. But each day the echoes from his conscience came back weaker and his arguments sounded flatter. He was losing the battle, convinced he was being swept away in the whirlpool with little control over what was happening to either of them. For the most part Rush had given up the struggle and was living one day at a time, spending time with Lindy, savoring the moments they were together. But he couldn't, wouldn't allow the fickle Fates to carry him where they would, knowing full well they'd place him with Lindy, warm and willing, in his bed.

Jeff Dwyer knew him well enough to have guessed something had changed Rush's life. The day before Jeff had confronted Rush and suggested that he revealed all the symptoms of a man in love. Rush had denied that, probably a lot more forcefully than he should have, because Jeff had gone on to enumerate the changes he'd seen in Rush since the *Mitchell*'s arrival back in Bremerton.

Not willing to drop the matter, Jeff had shown up at the apartment. He seemed to take delight in informing Rush that he'd been watching him closely of late. Jeff had noticed how quickly Rush left work the minute his shift was over, as if he couldn't wait to get back to his apartment. It used to be that Rush hung around awhile to shoot the bull with the other guys. No more. Rush was out of the shipyard like greased lightning. And furthermore, Jeff had claimed, Rush walked around with a cocky half smile, as though he found something highly amusing. As far as Jeff was concerned, these telltale symptoms added up to one thing: a woman.

Rush hadn't argued with his friend. He'd simply

refused to discuss the subject. A lot of good it had done him. Just when he'd thought he was making headway and Jeff was about to drop the entire matter, Lindy had come bursting in the front door. Her eyes had glowed and sparkled as they sought him, confirming everything Jeff had been saying ten times over.

At his side, Lindy roared to her feet cheering. Lost in his thoughts, Rush hadn't been watching the game and now he saw that the Mariners had just scored. He joined Lindy and shouted once for effect.

Lindy laughed gleefully, turned to him and hugged his waist, her eyes alive with joy. With hardly a pause, she sat back down and reached for the bag of peanuts. Rush took his seat as well, but his mind was whirling. He wanted to kiss Lindy at that moment, and the need was so strong in him that it demanded all his restraint not to haul her into his arms right then and there. He reached for the peanuts himself and noted grimly that his hands were trembling with the need to touch her.

The game must have gotten good, because several times during the next few innings Lindy scooted to the edge of her seat and shouted advice to both player and umpire. As far as Rush could tell, he'd responded appropriately throughout the game. He'd cheered and hissed a couple of times, applauded and booed when Lindy did, but he hadn't a clue what was going on in the field. Dealing with what was happening to his own emotions was all he could handle for now. He was plowing through mine-infested waters with Lindy, and he was gradually losing his grip on his control with each minute he spent in her company.

Following the baseball game they walked from the Kingdome back to the apartment, a healthy two miles. Personally he would have preferred a taxi, but Lindy was in a mood to walk. She chatted as they strolled along, hand in hand. She was pleased that the home team had won and soon Rush felt himself caught up in her good mood.

Lindy didn't know what was wrong with Rush, but he hadn't been himself all evening. He'd hardly spoken during the entire game, and although he seemed to be paying attention, she could have sworn he hadn't noticed a blasted thing.

For her part, Lindy felt great. More than great. She felt wonderful! And so much of this newly dis-covered inner peace was due to loving Rush. She even knew the precise minute she'd recognized the truth about her feelings for her brother's friend. It had been the morning of her first day at Boeing, when he'd told her he couldn't let her think he'd touched another woman after kissing her. Even now, the memory of his words had the power to bring tears to her eyes. For days she'd yearned to tell him how her life had changed since she'd met him. But her words would only embarrass him, so she'd kept them locked inside her heart until she was convinced she'd choke on them.

When they reached the apartment, Rush held open the door for her to precede him inside. Lindy stepped into the living room, but didn't turn on any lights. The view of the Seattle skyline from the window drew Lindy there.

"Isn't it lovely?" she said, looking out over the glimmering lights of the waterfront. All seventy-five floors of the Columbia Center were lit, as was the Smith Tower.

Rush stood behind her, but said nothing.

Lindy turned and slipped her arms around his middle, pressing her ear to his broad chest, hugging him, savoring the peace of the moment, knowing he wouldn't allow it to last long.

His lips brushed the top of her head and she smiled. From experience Lindy knew that he tensed before he kissed her, as though gathering together his reserve of self-control. True to form, he stiffened and she smiled because she was beginning to know him so well. Eager now, she raised her head and tilted it to one side to receive his kiss. As it had been on previous nights, his mouth was warm and moist as it glided smoothly over hers. In welcome she parted her lips and slipped her arms up his chest to lazily loop them around his neck.

His kiss was light. Petal soft. Controlled.

Already his hands were braced on her shoulders, cupping them as he prepared to ease himself out of her arms. Lindy felt as though she were starving and a delectable feast was within easy reach, and yet Rush wouldn't allow her more than a sample.

''No,'' she objected in a tight whisper. She raised her hands to touch his face, her fingertips gliding over his features, hoping to memorize each one, burn it into her heart so that when he left her she could bear the parting.

''Lindy, don't,'' he groaned, and squeezed his eyes closed. He gripped her wrists and brought her fingers to his lips, kissing the tips.

''Hold me for just a little while longer.'' She thought for a moment that he was going to argue with her, but he didn't. With her arms draped around his neck, she pressed her cheek over his and felt him relax ever so slightly. But it wasn't nearly enough to satisfy her, and unable to resist, she turned her head and nuzzled his ear with her nose. Her mouth grazed his clenched jaw. Her lips worked their way across his brow, over his eyes and down the side of his nose to nibble on his lower lip. She hesitated, then ran the moist tip of her tongue over the seam of his lips.

Rush's arms tightened around her and he whispered her name on the tail end of a plea for her to stop.

He wanted her. She could feel the evidence boldly

pressing against her thigh, and the knowledge of his desire gave her a heady sense of power. Led by instinct, she edged as close as possible to him and rotated her hips once, biting back a cry at the pleasure the action gave her even as it created a need for more. So much more.

"Oh God," he moaned through clenched teeth. "Lindy, don't do that."

"All I want you to do is hold me for a few minutes more. Is that so much to ask?"

"Yes," he returned, and his breath came in hot, quick gasps.

If he had planned on arguing with her, he didn't follow through—apparently having decided it was a losing battle. His hands, which until that moment had been on either side of her waist, moved slowly upward as though drawn there by a force stronger than his will.

Lindy's breasts strained against the fabric of her T-shirt with the need to experience his touch. Slowly his palms encircled her breasts, cupping them, weighing her ripe fullness.

Her soft moans echoed his.

"Lindy, no," he breathed, and the words seemed to stagger from his lips, low and reluctant. "Tell me to stop. Remind me what a good friend your brother is." His thumbs rotated around her nipples, which beaded into hard pebbles and stood proudly at attention. Rush groaned once more.

He kissed her then, hard, thrusting his tongue deep into her mouth as if to punish her for making him want her so desperately. She used her hands to hold his head as her eager tongue met his and they dueled and stroked against each other.

He broke away from her and sucked in deep, uneven breaths. "This has got to stop," he whispered fervently into her hair. "Now."

Lindy found she could say nothing. She searched his handsome face for some sign, anything that would explain why it was so urgent for them to stop kissing when she felt so right in his arms. Her heart was pounding in a hard, fast rhythm that made her feel breathless and weak.

Yet at the same time she was filled with an awesome sense of power. Standing on tiptoe, she slanted her mouth over his and used her tongue to torment him, probing his mouth with swift, gentle thrusts.

"Oh God, Lindy." He kissed her then, firmly, leaving her in no doubt that he was the one in control, not she.

Without Lindy being sure how he'd managed it, Rush had her T-shirt off and her bra unfastened and discarded. The next thing Lindy knew, they were both on the sofa, she in a reclining position, Rush above her. He kissed her face, her forehead, her eyes and lips, again and again, until she lost count. Then his mouth worked its way down the delicate line of her jaw to her neck. She sucked in a wobbly breath when his moist, hot lips found one of her nipples and drew it into his mouth for his tongue to torment. When he'd finished with it he moved to the other nipple, licking it until it ached and throbbed, taut and firm.

He kissed her lips repeatedly, and waves of erotic sensation lapped over her like water pounding relentlessly against the shore.

Lindy was throbbing everywhere. Her mouth, her tongue, her breasts, her belly and the area between her thighs. Her fingers wove their way through his hair.

"Rush." She whispered his name in a tormented whisper. "I love you so much."

He stilled, and after a torturous moment he raised his head. Poised as he was above her, his eyes feasted on her, studying her for what seemed an eternity. Then he shook himself as though coming out of a mindless fog. "You don't mean that. You don't know what you're saying."

"I know exactly what I'm saying." She held his head with her hands and said it again. "I love you." She punctuated each word with a swift kiss on his lips.

Rush's brow folded into a dark, brooding frown. "You can't possibly mean that. Lindy, for God's sake, you barely know me!"

"I know everything I need to." She smiled up at

him, not willing to listen to any more of his arguments.

As though he wasn't sure how to respond, Rush slowly disentangled their limbs one by one, the whole time looking as if he didn't have a clue how they'd ended up that way. When he'd finished, he sat on the edge of the sofa and wiped a hand back and forth over his face.

"Lindy, listen."

"No. I'm not going to because you're going to argue with me, and I won't let you." She sat upright, their thighs so close they touched.

"It's only natural...."

Lindy slid off the sofa and pressed one knee to the floor so she could look him in the eye, but his gaze stubbornly refused to meet hers.

"I know exactly what you're going to say."

His face was tight with what looked like embarrassment as he reached for her T-shirt and handed it to her. Lindy smiled and slipped it over her head.

"I love you," she repeated, feeling more sure of herself every time she said it.

"Lindy...."

"I'm not too young to know my own mind." When his gaze shot to her, she knew she'd stumbled over one of his objections. "I'm twenty-two years old, for heaven's sake. I'm not a child."

He opened his mouth to argue with her, but she pressed her finger over his lips to silence him. "Now this is the biggie. You're worried about what happened with Paul and you think all this emotion I feel for you has to do with him. I can understand your concern, and in the beginning you might have been right. But not now. I was mulling this over the other night. Thinking about how low I was when I moved to Seattle and how I was convinced nothing good would ever happen to me again. Then I met you, and, Rush..." she stopped, biting into her bottom lip as the emotion filled her eyes.

"There's no need...."

"Yes, there is." Her hands cupped his face, her gaze delving into his, showing him all the love that came shining through from her heart. "When I think about everything that led me to move to Seattle I haven't a single regret. Not one. All the pain, all the disillusionment was worth it. In fact, I'll always be grateful to Paul because it was through him that I found you."

"Lindy, stop. Don't say any more."

"But I have to. Don't you see?"

Rush closed his eyes and pressed his cheek next to her tear-stained one. His breathing was as labored as her own, but otherwise he didn't move.

"It took what happened with Paul for me to find you, appreciate you, understand you. I love you so much.... I can't keep it inside anymore."

"Oh, Lord, don't say that."

Once more, she pressed her finger over his lips.

"I don't want anything from you. Nothing. You didn't ask for this, and I've probably embarrassed the hell out of you by blurting it out. I apologize, but Rush—my noble, honorable Rush—I do love you."

She stood then, her legs a little shaky. "Having gotten that off my chest, I'm going to leave you."

"Lindy?" His gruff voice stopped her.

"Yes?"

He had the look of a man who'd been pulled apart on a torture rack. He rubbed a hand down over his face and then shook his head. "Nothing."

The following morning Lindy woke to hear Rush rummaging around the kitchen, albeit quietly, no doubt hoping to escape without having to confront her. She climbed out of bed and greeted him with a warm smile.

"'Morning."

He grumbled something in return.

"Did you sleep well?"

He gave her a look that told her he hadn't. "I've got watch today."

"Yes, I know."

"It's Saturday. How come you aren't sleeping in?"

She dropped her eyes. "I wanted to be sure of something."

"What?"

"That you believe what I told you last night."

His gaze found hers and Lindy could tell he was struggling within himself. The stern look he wore so often in the morning softened somewhat, but when he spoke his voice remained gruff. "Listen, I'm not much of a conversationalist at this time of day, and now probably isn't the best place to discuss this." He paused as though to compose his thoughts, sighed and then continued. "I want you to know, I'm truly flattered that you think you love me."

"But—"

"But," he cut in, "you can't trust what you're feeling right now. So let's leave it at that. Okay?"

"Leave it?" she flared. "Rush, no...."

"I'll be your friend, Lindy, but that's all I ever intend to be."

"My friend?"

"And that's it, so don't argue." He downed the last of his coffee and set the cup in the sink with as much force as if he intended to shove it down the drain. "I'll see you later."

"Okay. If that's the way you want it."

"I do."

"Then I'd be honored to have you for a friend, Rush Callaghan."

He paused, his back to her. "No more kissing, Lindy. I mean that."

"No kissing," she echoed.

"We're going to live as brother and sister from here on out."

"Brother and sister." Lindy knew that would last until about lunchtime tomorrow, if that long.

"And if it proves too difficult for us, then I'll make arrangements to live aboard the *Mitchell*."

"If you think it's for the best," she agreed, doing her best to swallow her amusement. Rush's reaction was exactly as she'd guessed it would be. "If that's what you honestly want."

His hand slammed against the counter. "You know it isn't," he said, and whirled around to face her. "Damn it all to hell. Have you the slightest notion of how close we came to making love last night?"

She nodded.

"I've never known a woman who could tie me into knots the way you do. I promised myself I wasn't going to touch you again, and here it is seven-thirty in the morning and I want you so damn much I hurt."

Silently she stepped to his side and looked up at him, her eyes wide and innocent.

"Damn it, Lindy," he groaned. "Why do you have to be so beautiful?" He slipped his arms around her waist and exhaled sharply. "Now kiss me before I go. I'll be back as soon as I can."

Obediently she twined her arms around his neck and raised her lips to his. "Anything you say, big brother."

Chapter 7

Freshly ground hamburger squished between Lindy's long fingers as she meshed the meat and spices together to form patties for the barbecue grill. It was a lovely summer afternoon in a week that had begun with such marvelous promise.

The front door opened and Rush let himself in to the apartment.

"Hi," Lindy called out, pleased to see him. He was fifteen minutes later than usual, and she'd hoped he hadn't missed the ferry, which ran hourly. "How do barbecued hamburgers sound for dinner?"

"Fine."

The word was clipped and impatient, as though what she served for their evening meal was the least of his concerns. Surprised at his gruff tone, Lindy turned around to find him standing in the doorway, his brow furrowed in a frown so tight it darkened his face.

"Did you have a bad day?"

"No."

Something was obviously troubling him, but from the hard set of his mouth, she knew it wouldn't do her any good to ask. In an effort to ignore his surly mood, she hurried to tell him her good news. "I got word from Steve. The *Atlantis* is due in as early as next week."

Rush acknowledged the information with a curt nod.

"There's cold pop in the fridge if that interests you."

Apparently it didn't because Rush left her and moved into the living room to turn on the television. Lindy finished her task, washed the hamburger goop from her fingers and joined him there, sitting on the arm of the sofa. She rested her elbow gently on Rush's shoulder while Susan Hutchinson from Channel 7 relayed the latest news-making incident from the Persian Gulf.

When Rush pulled out of Bremerton, Lindy knew the *Mitchell* would be headed for those same trouble-infested waters. Her heart thudded heavily in her chest as she battled to control her anxiety. She hated to think of Rush in any danger and wished the

Mitchell was headed for the South Pacific or somewhere equally pleasant.

Rush must have sensed her fears because he wrapped his arm around her and gently squeezed her waist. Her hand slid over his shoulder and she kissed the top of his head, loving him more each minute of every day.

"Lindy?"

"Hmm?"

The tension in his shoulders was so severe, she wondered how he could hold himself stiff for so long and still breathe.

"When I leave, I don't want you clinging to me."

She blinked, not sure she understood what he was saying. He seemed to be implying she would make a scene on the dock, weeping and gnashing her teeth because the man she loved was heading out to sea. That he would even imagine such a thing was an insult. The other implication was even more offensive.

"Are you suggesting that once you leave I should start dating other men?"

A week seemed to pass before he answered. "Yes. I think that would be a good idea."

Lindy was slow to react to what he was suggesting. Her emotions went from surprise to mild irritation, then quickly broadened to out-and-out fury. She jerked her arm off his shoulder and leaped to her feet. "Well, thank you very much."

"For what?"

If it hadn't been so tragic, so painfully sad, Lindy might have laughed. She'd never felt as close to any man as she had to Rush these past two weeks. When she'd declared her love, she hadn't been looking for white lace and promises. The words had been seared against her tender heart and she hadn't been able to hold them inside a minute longer. She hadn't asked anything of him, but she certainly hadn't expected this intolerable pat on the hand, telling her she was too young, too immature or too stupid to know her own mind.

"For God's sake, think about it, will you?"

"What?" she returned in like voice. "That I'm still a baby and certainly incapable of sound judgment? How about the fact that I'm looking to prove myself after Paul? What I feel for you is obviously some rebounding thing to soothe my injured ego. Right? Is that what you want me to think about, Rush? Unfortunately I can't come up with a single reason I should, since you've already shoved those things in my face at every opportunity."

His jaw was clenched so hard that his temple went white. "You're fresh out of college...."

"And still tied to Mama's apron strings. Is that what you mean to imply?"

"No."

Oh, the gall of the man. Rather than continue arguing, Lindy returned to the kitchen. She was so furious that she clenched her hands into hard fists and exhaled several times to gain control of her simmering rage. She gritted her teeth as she went about fixing their meal. If Rush was so keen for her to start dating someone, then Lindy could see no reason why she should wait until the *Mitchell* left Puget Sound. A small sense of satisfaction lifted the corner of her mouth in a soft sneer as she thought about having men come to the apartment to pick her up and the pleasure she'd derive from introducing them to Rush. Oh, he'd really love that. She might even stay the night with a friend from work and let Rush stew, thinking she was with another man. Then she'd see exactly how eager he was to have her meet someone else.

Lindy braced her hands against the counter and hung her head in abject defeat. Behaving that way was childish and immature and impossibly stupid. Sure, she'd make Rush suffer, but *she* would end up being the one with a broken heart and myriad regrets.

Rush seemed to be telling her something more. Yes, he hungered for her physically. The circumstances in which they were living were rife with sexual tension. Each day it became more difficult to ignore the fire between them, and more than once they'd gotten close enough to the flames to singe their self-control.

The realization hit Lindy then, the impact as

strong as if Rush had slugged his fist into her stomach. In some ways it would have been easier if he had. Rush didn't love her. He pitied her after what had happened with Paul. All his tenderness, all his concern, everything he'd done had been born of pity. She'd mistaken his touch, his soul-wrenching kisses for passion when, from the beginning, all he'd really felt was compassion for her.

"Where's my book?"

Rush's question came at her as if from outer space. She turned to discover he stood not more than five feet away, looking irritated and impatient. She hadn't a clue what he was talking about.

"My book?" he repeated. "The one that was in the living room last night. What did you do with it?"

Still numb, she raised her hand and pointed toward his bedroom. "I set it on your dresser."

Since there was so little time in the morning, Lindy had gotten into the habit of straightening up the apartment before she went to bed. The night before Rush had been at a meeting, and she'd retired early, tired from a long day, before he'd gotten home.

"I'd appreciate it if you left my things alone," Rush said in a low growl. "Move whatever you want of yours, but kindly keep your hands off mine."

Answering him with anything more than a shake

of her head would have been impossible. Lindy didn't know what had gone wrong, but in the space of fifteen minutes her world had been badly shaken. First Rush had told her he wanted her to start seeing other men and then he'd jumped all over her for putting his book away. Nothing seemed to make sense anymore.

The insight came to her then—it seemed to be the night for them—Rush wanted her out of the apartment. When she'd gotten the job with Boeing, it had been understood she'd need to wait for a couple of paychecks before she could afford to rent her own place. They hadn't actually discussed it, and at the time Lindy had let the subject drop because she'd wanted to spend as much time as she could with Rush. He hadn't asked her about it, and she'd assumed that he wanted her with him just as much. Once more, she'd been wrong.

Quickly calculating her limited funds, she realized that with what remained of her savings and her first check, which was due on Friday, she could possibly afford a studio apartment. If she asked around at the office, there might even be someone there who was looking for a roommate.

The muscles in her throat constricted as she fought down the regret. She'd been such a fool.

Rush noted that Lindy left the apartment as soon as she'd finished preparing their dinner, not both-

ering to eat anything herself. For that matter he
didn't have much of an appetite either, but he sat
down at the table, propped his book open in front
of him and pretended an interest in both the book
and the dinner.

It had been on the tip of his tongue to ask Lindy
where she was going, but he'd swallowed the question, realizing how stupid it would sound after the
way he'd laid into her earlier. He hadn't meant to
start a fight, hadn't even been looking for one. It
had just happened, and he was as shocked by his
insensitive demands as Lindy had been. He hadn't
meant a thing he'd said. The hurt in her expressive
dark eyes returned to haunt him now. When he'd
asked her about the book, she'd stood looking at him
in confusion, the violet smudges that appeared beneath her eyes a silent testimony to the trauma his
words had inflicted.

As for the suggestion she see other men, that was
downright idiotic. Talk about inflicting self-torture!
He wanted to see Lindy with another man about as
much as he desired a bladder infection.

The problem, Rush knew, was that he loved
Lindy Kyle. She was stubborn, headstrong, proud…
warm and vibrant. She might as well have branded
his heart, because he belonged to her.

Rush pushed his plate aside and wearily wiped a
palm across his eyes. Hell, this was the last thing
he'd planned would happen. He was thirty-two years

old, for God's sake. Mature enough to recognize when he was headed for trouble. He'd known what was going to happen with Lindy from the first night he'd seen her standing, all soft and feminine, in the hallway outside Steve's bedroom. He'd known the morning she'd blasted the rock music loud enough to hurl him out of bed because she was hurt and angry. He'd known when she'd held his head between her hands and stared into his soul and whispered so sweetly that she loved him.

Rush stood and walked out onto the lanai, hands buried in his pants pockets. The dark green waters of Puget Sound were visible and Rush snickered softly. So much for not seeking a bridge to tie him to the mainland. He was trapped on shore now and he dreaded leaving. He used to think of the navy as the only wife he'd ever need. But recently, when he crawled into bed at night, it was Lindy he longed to wrap his arms around. Lindy he longed to love. He wanted her to be a permanent part of his life. She was laughter and sunshine. She'd made him feel again, laugh again, love again. He couldn't bear to think of what the future would be like without her. Two weeks. He'd only been with Lindy for two weeks. Before that she'd been a name, the sister of a good friend. He couldn't ask her to share his life based on a two-week acquaintance. It was crazy. No, he'd be patient with her, force himself to wait. The six-month separation would do them both good.

Time would test the strength of their love. Time would reveal the truth.

It was only a little after eight-thirty when Lindy returned to the apartment. She would have preferred to stay away much longer, but after reading through the evening newspaper for apartment rentals and wasting five dollars on a horrible movie she didn't know where else to go or what else to do. Eventually she'd need to return anyway, and knowing Rush, he'd probably left the apartment, as well.

He wasn't in the living room or kitchen, and she didn't bother to check any of the other rooms, not wanting a recurrence of their earlier argument. It was obvious he wasn't in the mood for company.

Sitting at the table, Lindy spread out the classified section and read the apartment-for-rent advertisements once more.

Quite by accident she found a section she hadn't thought to look at before: roommates wanted. She read a couple of those and decided to phone the one that looked the most promising.

"Hello," she said brightly when the woman answered. "I'm calling about your ad in the paper."

Rush walked into the kitchen, hesitated when he saw her and opened the refrigerator to take out a cold can of pop. Lindy strove to ignore him as much as possible. Her fingers gripped the pen unnecessarily hard as she doodled while the woman on the other end of the line explained a few of the details regarding her ad.

"It says here that you're looking for a nonsmoker. I...I don't smoke and I've recently moved into the area and need a place to live. I...have a job."

"Lindy."

Rush called her name, but she pretended she hadn't heard him. Besides she was already involved in one conversation and if he chose to be rude that was his problem.

Undeterred, Rush waved his hand in front of her face. "Get off the phone."

"Excuse me a minute please." Lindy spoke to the woman, enunciating each word as she held her temper by a fragile thread. She pressed the receiver to her shoulder blade and glared up at Rush. "Just what do you think you're doing?" she hissed between clenched teeth.

"There's no need for you to find an apartment," he told her, returning her heated stare.

"I beg your pardon, Rush Callaghan, but this is my life, and if I choose to leave this apartment, I'll do so with or without your permission."

Rush cursed beneath his breath and walked away from her.

"I'm sorry to keep you waiting," Lindy said sweetly into the telephone receiver. "Perhaps it would be best if we met?"

"Damn it, Lindy," Rush shouted, twisting around

to face her once more. "Will you kindly get off the phone so we can talk?"

He might as well have been speaking to a stone wall for all the attention Lindy paid him. "Yes, Tuesday afternoon would be fine."

Rush's returning glare was hot enough to peel thirty-year-old wallpaper off a wall, but still Lindy ignored him.

"You won't be meeting whoever that is," he told her sternly, looming over her. "You're only wasting time."

"Kindly excuse me again, would you?" Lindy asked softly, deliberately calm. She turned to Rush then and half rose from her chair. "Would you shut up? I can't hear a word she's saying."

"Good."

He was making Lindy more furious by the minute, and she tried to tell him as much and still keep control of her temper. "I'm sorry to keep interrupting our conversation," she said to the woman on the phone.

Rush walked around the table a couple of times, looking like a man trapped in a small space—or a shark circling its kill. Finally he stopped, standing directly across from her. He closed his eyes and rubbed a hand along the back of his neck as though to relieve an ache there, then paused and looked at her. "Lindy, I'm leaving."

The words were nearly shouted. She hesitated and

prayed for patience, and when that didn't work, she counted to ten. Flippantly she raised her hand and waved goodbye. Still, he didn't move.

"I'm twenty-two," Lindy answered the woman's question. "No...no you needn't worry about that sort of thing. There isn't anyone important in my life at the moment." She swallowed tightly at the lie.

She exchanged a look with Rush and feared he was going to explode. "I thought you were leaving," she whispered heatedly, cupping her hand over the mouthpiece. "Don't let me stop you."

"Not the apartment," he raged, staring at her as though she were completely dense. "The *Mitchell* is sailing out."

"I know.... In two weeks."

"The catapults are being tested tomorrow and possibly Wednesday. If everything works out we'll be gone by the beginning of next week."

"The beginning of next week," she echoed, hanging up the phone. She kept her hand on the receiver feeling numb with shock, numb with fear. "But you said it would be at least a month."

"As I recall, I told you it could be as long as a month. As it happens, it's only two, possibly three weeks."

"Oh, Rush." She turned to him, her eyes wide with a hundred emotions she didn't know how to define. She'd accepted long ago that their time together was limited. But she'd counted on every minute of these remaining weeks. Needed them. Needed Rush.

"It shouldn't come as any great surprise," he told her, and pulled out a chair to sit across from her.

"It isn't.... It's just that... I don't know." Her stomach twisted into hard knots and for a painful moment she couldn't breathe. She was stunned, and she felt Rush's eyes slowly search her face. With everything in her, she met his gaze, determined to appear cool and composed. Her heart might be quivering with apprehension, but she'd die smiling before she'd allow him to know it. He'd already told her once that he didn't want her clinging to him when he left. And she wouldn't. She'd stand on the dock with a smile on her lips and a tear in her eye, and wave until her arm dropped off, but she'd never let him know it was killing her.

"About tonight," he started again. "I didn't mean any of what I said."

He dropped his gaze, but not before Lindy saw a strange mixture of regret, desire and remorse. In the two weeks they'd been together, Lindy had thought she'd witnessed all Rush's moods. She'd seen him at his cynical best, when he'd been purposely aloof and brash. She'd experienced his comfort, his tenderness as he held her in his arms while she sobbed against his chest. And she'd heard the music of his laughter, stood transfixed by his sometimes warm-heated, playful moods. Oh Lord, she was going to miss him. Miss everything about him.

"Lindy, I'm sorry for what I said."

His hand reached for hers, rubbing warmth back into her chilled fingers. She shook her head, hoping that would suffice as acceptance of his apology.

They were silent for a moment, caught in the surging tide of their individual thoughts.

"I don't have any right to ask you to wait six months for me."

"I'll wait," she offered quietly. Lindy had no other choice.

"If you meet someone else..."

"Is that what you want?"

"No." Anger flared briefly in his eyes. Then his expression changed to that cool, watchful look he wore so often. "No," he repeated softly.

"That isn't what you said earlier." She tried to laugh, but the sound of her pain was carried in the mirth.

"I didn't mean it. Not a word."

"You don't believe that I love you, do you?"

He waited a long time before he answered. "I don't know. I think it's too soon after Paul for you to know what you're feeling."

Lindy closed her eyes in an effort to control the urge to argue with him. She did love him, and never more than now. She'd just learned he'd be sailing out of her life for half a year, and her only thought was how she would manage without him.

She watched as a small pulse started in his temple. "I don't want to leave you, Lindy."

Her gaze shot to his, and her eyes widened with astonishment. Rush loved the sea. The navy was more than his career. It was his life, the very reason he got out of bed every morning. She'd listened for hours while he described for her the warm sensations that went through him when he was on the open seas. She'd felt his pride and exhilaration when he spoke of standing alone against the force of a fierce storm. He loved everything about navy life. It was his dream, just as the oceans of the world were his destiny.

And he didn't want to leave her. What he felt for her was stronger than the lure of the sea.

Tears shimmered in her eyes and she bit hard on her lower lip to hold them at bay. Rush wouldn't tell her he loved her—not with words. It would have been more than she could expect. But by admitting that he didn't want to leave her, he said everything.

When Lindy had composed herself enough to look up at Rush again, she felt the tension in every line of his lovingly familiar face.

"I want you to stay at the apartment," he said, and his hand continued to rub hers, holding her fingers in a grip that was almost painfully tight. "Steve will be back soon, but he'll only be here a few weeks, if that long.

Lindy nodded.

"Then the place will be empty for months."

Again she acknowledged his words with an abrupt movement of her head.

"It would be better if there was someone living here. As it is now, an empty apartment is an invitation to burglars. You'd actually be doing Steve and me a favor if you agree to say."

"I'll...I'll want to start contributing toward the rent."

"Fine. Whatever you want. When Steve arrives the two of you can work it out."

"What about when Steve is here?" Lindy asked. "Where will I sleep?"

"He can have my room."

"But what about when you're both here?"

Rush frowned, and then a strange, almost humorous light entered his eyes and a soft smile crowded his face. "Let's cross that bridge when we get to it. Okay?"

"Okay."

"Anything else?" he asked.

She dropped her gaze to his hand, which was holding hers. "I love you, Rush, and I'm going to miss you like hell."

He raised her hand to his lips, closed his eyes and kissed it gently.

* * *

The coffee was ready by the time Rush met Lindy in the kitchen the following morning. Although she'd been physically and mentally exhausted, she'd hardly slept, managing three, maybe four hours of rest at the most. Now her eyes burned and she felt on the verge of tears.

Rush joined her at the table. He wordlessly reached for the morning newspaper and buried his face in it, not speaking to her—apparently pretending she wasn't there. Lindy stood it as long as she could.

"Would you like some breakfast?" she asked.

He shook his head. The stupid newspaper still presented a thin barrier between them.

Whereas Lindy had felt loved and reassured after their talk the night before, this morning she felt lonely and bereft. Rush hadn't sailed away yet, but he might as well have for all the companionship he offered.

"I think I'll get dressed now," she whispered, hoping that would gain his attention.

"Fine."

"Stop it, Rush."

That worked, and he lowered the paper, peering at her over the top of the page, his face clean of expression. "Stop what?"

"That!" She pointed an accusing finger at the newspaper. "I hate it when you do this."

"What hideous crime am I guilty of now?"

"You haven't left yet.... I'd think you'd want to spend every minute you could with me.... Instead you're hiding behind the *Post-Intelligencer* so you won't have to look at me."

"You're being ridiculous."

"I'm not. It's almost as if you can hardly wait to get away from me."

With deliberately slow movements he folded the newspaper and set it aside. "Is it because I didn't want any breakfast? Is that what's upset you so much? You know I seldom eat this early."

"No...of course that's not it."

"What is it then?"

"I...don't know." Lindy felt like such a fool. She didn't know why she was acting like this, but she couldn't stand it when Rush treated her this way. She could deal with his anger far more easily than this intolerable patience.

"What exactly do you want from me, Lindy?"

"I want some emotion," she cried.

"What?" he barked, clearly not understanding her.

"Not tears. I want you to...oh, never mind. Go back to reading your precious paper with that same stoic expression you always wear in the morning. I humbly apologize for having interrupted your reading time."

Lindy couldn't get to her bedroom fast enough.

She took small pleasure in slamming her door. Her intention had been to dress as quickly as she could and leave the apartment. Instead she found herself sitting on the edge of her bed, trembling and teary eyed, confused and suddenly feeling, utterly, desperately alone.

When her bedroom door flew open, Lindy gasped. Rush's gaze pinned her to the bed as he silently stalked across the room.

"Damn it, Lindy." The words were ground out through his teeth before he sank onto the bed beside her. His arms tightened around her trembling body, pressing her down against the mattress. His hands found and cupped her breasts as he buried his face in her hair, spreading a wildfire of kisses along her cheeks and face, but avoiding her lips.

All Rush had to do was touch her and the desire curled in her belly like an anchor rope ready to plunge her into dark, inviting depths of passion.

His fingers tightened on her shoulders as he raised his head and stared down at her. He looked as though he were trying to stop himself but couldn't. Then his mouth closed hungrily over hers, rubbing back and forth, his tongue probing hers.

Lindy's arms found his back and she arched her spine, grinding her hips against him, needing him so desperately she could barely breathe. The longer Rush kissed her, the deeper she sank into the turbulent waters of desire. She felt like she was drowning, oblivious to everything except the primitive need to be loved by Rush.

"Oh, Lindy...." The words came out softly as he lifted his head from hers. He paused and dragged in a heavy breath, held it a moment then expelled it. "Well," he whispered, "is that enough emotion for you?"

Chapter 8

Lindy liked Susan Dwyer the minute the two met. Susan's reddish-brown hair was naturally curly, and although it was styled fashionably short, it managed to fall in an unruly array surrounding her pert face. She possessed the largest, liveliest brown eyes that Lindy could ever remember seeing on anyone. They sparkled with intelligence and vitality, glinting with warmth and curiosity as they studied Lindy.

"Jeff has talked of little else since he met you the other day," Susan confessed.

"It was certainly nice of you to invite Rush and me over for dinner," Lindy returned. Twin boys, about eighteen months of age with reddish caps of curly hair like their mother's stood at the edge of their playpen, silently regarding the two women through large, doleful brown eyes. They'd recently awakened from a late-afternoon nap and looked mournfully toward Susan in the hope that she'd abandon her dinner guests and play with them.

"A meal is a small price to pay to meet you."

Lindy smiled at that. "I take it Rush hasn't said much about me?"

"Are you kidding? He's been so tight-mouthed one would think you were top-secret information."

"That sounds like Rush." Lindy's gaze sought him out and found him and Jeff on the back patio, lighting up the barbecue grill. Just watching him gave her a solid, warm feeling deep inside her breast. She'd found him attractive before, but now, set against this low-key social background, dressed casually in jeans and a striped shirt, looking relaxed and at ease, she found she loved him all the more.

"Rush and Jeff have been friends a lot of years," Susan went on to say. She opened the refrigerator, brought out a large bowl of potato salad and set it on the kitchen counter. "Jeff knew the first day after the *Mitchell* returned that something had happened to Rush. He mentioned it to me right away, but it wasn't until last week that he knew that Rush had found a special woman."

"Rush is the one who's special." Lindy continued to study him, trying to put the knowledge that he'd be leaving out of her mind long enough to enjoy this one evening with his friends.

Susan turned around and her gaze followed Lindy's. "He's happier now than I can ever remember seeing him. More serene. You've been good for him, Lindy—really good. I didn't used to like Rush.... Actually I was only reciprocating what he felt toward me. I think I may have reminded him of someone he knew a long time ago. Although Jeff's never told me this, I believe Rush may have tried to talk him out of marrying me."

"I've never known a man who can frown the way he does," Lindy said with a soft sigh. "I swear one of those famous looks of his could curdle milk a block away."

Susan hooted. "I know exactly the look you mean."

"How long have you and Jeff been married?" From everything Rush had told Lindy about Susan, and he'd spoken of little else on the hour-long ferry ride to Bremerton, Rush held his friend's wife in the highest regard. She was surprised to hear he'd once felt differently.

"We've been married about two and a half years now."

Jeff said something that caused Rush to chuckle. The low, modulated laugh seemed to shoot into the sky. Then they both laughed.

Surprised, Lindy and Susan turned around.

"I don't think I've ever really heard Rush laugh quite like that.... So free," Susan murmured, as she gazed at the two men. "He's always been so cynical, so stoic. I never really knew what he was thinking. When we first met he terrified me."

"I know what you felt," Lindy said slowly. "The first couple of days after I met Rush, I found myself wanting to thwart him. He can be such an arrogant bastard."

"And at the same time there's something so appealing about him," Susan answered thoughtfully. "And I'm not talking about how good-looking he is, either, although God knows he's handsome enough. But even when he openly disapproved of me, I couldn't help admiring and respecting him. It took time to earn his trust, and despite everything I was glad he was Jeff's friend. There's something inherently strong about Rush. Strong and intensely loyal. I've always known Rush would look out for Jeff no matter what the circumstances. It helped when Jeff had to leave.... Knowing he would be with Rush."

"He's the Rock of Gibraltar, I know," Lindy answered softly, loving him so much her heart ached. "Loyal and constant." She tried not to think about the huge aircraft carrier sailing out of Bremerton, taking Rush thousands of miles away from her. She attempted to push away all thoughts of how empty her life would be after the *Mitchell* left.

"What's it like?" Lindy whispered, hardly aware the words had slipped from her mouth.

Intuitively, it seemed, Susan knew what she was asking. "I don't sleep for the first week. No matter how many times Jeff leaves, it's always the same. For seven days I lie in bed and stare at the ceiling, my stomach in knots. As much as I try I can't seem to stop fretting and worrying. Finally I'm so exhausted my body takes over, and I'm able to sleep."

"Rush told me you are one of the strongest women he knows…. The best kind of navy wife."

Susan's countenance softened and her cheeks flushed to a fetching shade of rose pink. She dipped her head a little and murmured, "How sweet of him to say so."

"What does Jeff say about your sleeping problems?" Lindy asked.

Susan shrugged. "He doesn't know."

"But…"

"He has enough worries and responsibilities aboard the *Mitchell* without me burdening him with more. As much as possible I send him off with a smile and handle anything that arises as best I can while he's gone."

"I'm afraid," Lindy admitted reluctantly. "Not because Rush is leaving; I…I can accept that. But I worry about them sailing in the Persian Gulf." Every night, it seemed, the news was filled with reports of violence in the troubled waters of the Middle East. Before they'd left the apartment she'd heard reports about gunboats that had attempted to attack the U.S. Naval forces that very afternoon. Lindy hadn't mentioned to Rush what she was feeling, knowing he'd brush off her concern. She wanted to be strong, wanted to be brave for both their sakes.

Susan's dark eyes clouded and her chin trembled just a little. "After what happened to the *Stark*, we're all concerned. You aren't alone. But if any of us wives were to dwell on the danger, we'd soon be basket cases. I try to put it out of my mind as much as I can. I believe in Jeff, too. He's damn good at what he does and he's part of the most advanced naval fleet in the world. My security rests in the fact that he can take care of himself and his men. Rush can, too."

"I haven't told Rush how afraid I am."

"Good." Susan's gentle smile was encouraging.

"I...love Rush." The words came out hoarse and broken. She didn't have the security Susan and the other navy wives had. Rush had done nothing more than ask her to wait for him. At most, she could be considered his girlfriend, his sweetheart. "I don't want to lose him." She dropped her gaze and rubbed her open hands down the front of her jeans, more fearful than ever over what the future could hold. "I've only known him two weeks.... I can't believe I feel this strongly."

"It was like that with Jeff and me. We married within a month after we met, and he left for six months in the South Pacific almost immediately afterward. Talk about worry!"

"But I thought that area was relatively peaceful."

Susan cast an affectionate look toward her husband. "It wasn't that. I...I was more concerned about how attractive Jeff would find those lovely Polynesian girls."

"Oh." Lindy hadn't thought of that.

Susan blushed a little. "I was pregnant at the time, feeling completely miserable and about as sexy as a tuna casserole. Naturally we didn't know it was twins and I was desperately sick every morning. The highlight of each day was when the mail was delivered. I'd wait all morning and pray there'd be a letter from Jeff. When one finally did arrive, Jeff wrote in detail, telling me about this erotic show he and Rush had managed to see while on shore leave on a small island whose name I can't even pronounce. Topless dancers and the whole bit. I was so upset I cried for days, convinced he didn't love me anymore, and if he did that he'd never want to make love to me again." She pressed her hands over her small breasts. "In case you haven't noticed, I'm not exactly richly endowed in that area."

"I'm not exactly Dolly Parton myself."

They laughed together in an easy camaraderie, as

if they'd known each other for a long time instead of just a few short hours.

"Anyway, I didn't write back. Every time I thought about him gawking at those other women and their gorgeous boobs, I got all the more furious. Here I was, heaving my guts out every morning and my loyal, true-blue husband was living it up on shore leave on some exotic island and writing home about how randy he was."

"I don't blame you for not writing back. I'm not sure I would have, either."

"Oh, Lindy," Susan said, pressing her hand on Lindy's forearm, her eyes wide and serious. "It was a terrible thing to do. Jeff about went crazy. He didn't know what had happened to me, and I think it nearly broke him mentally. I got the most soul-wrenching, tormented letter from him, begging me to let him know what had happened. His mind had worked everything into such a terrible state that he was convinced I'd lost the baby—we didn't know it was *babies* then—or even that I might have left him for another man. When I finally wrote and told him how unhappy I was that he'd gone to a stupid top-less show he made me promise never, ever to do anything like that to him again."

"Was Jeff here when Timmy and Tommy were born?"

Hearing their names mentioned, the twins cooed and stamped their feet, wanting out of their playpen prison. Susan was busy putting the finishing touches on the relish plate, so Lindy lifted first one and then the other, balancing them on her hips. The two were an armful, but Lindy managed, briefly wondering how Susan coped with them twenty-four hours a day.

"It worked out that Jeff was home for the birth, but we were lucky because he was scheduled for sea trials on my due date. The boys obliged us by arriving ten days early."

Timmy wound his fingers through Lindy's hair while Tommy took pleasure in playing with the spaghetti strap of her summer top.

"Rush is the boys' godfather," Susan explained. "The only times I've ever seen him let down his guard were with them—and then tonight with you. He'd make a wonderful father someday."

"I think he would, too," Lindy said, kissing the chubby cheek of each twin. The boys laughed and Timmy tried to lean over and grab a pickle from his mother's hands.

"Just a minute, son," Susan told him. "Dinner's almost ready."

To keep the pair entertained until their mother dished up their dinner plates, Lindy bounced them up and down on her hips in a jaunty, trotting step around the kitchen. She was laughing, her face flushed and happy, when she looked up to discover

Rush standing on the other side of the sliding glass door, watching her.

His deep blue eyes were so intense that her breath caught in her throat. Lindy thought for a moment that she might have done something to anger him. His gaze had narrowed, but there was a light shining from it that didn't speak of anger, but of something else, something far stronger that she couldn't define. A muscle worked in his cheek, and he seemed to be taking in every detail of her as she bounced the chubby cherubs on her hips.

Jeff must have called him because Rush turned abruptly and left without saying a word.

"Here, I'll take one of the boys," Susan offered, lifting Tommy from Lindy's hip. She carried the squirming child outside where two high chairs were positioned side by side next to the round picnic table.

Lindy followed her onto the patio and slipped Timmy into his seat.

"I learned a long time ago that it's best to feed the boys before Jeff and I even try to eat."

Lindy noted Susan had dished up foods her young sons could eat with their hands: chicken legs, finger-Jell-O, pickles and potato chips made up the twins' meal.

"They're getting so independent. They make a terrible fuss if I try to spoon-feed them anymore."

"Can they feed themselves?"

"For the most part." Susan was busy strapping in each toddler. "Believe me, it's a test of patience because more food lands on the floor and wall than ever makes it into their mouths. Afterward it's easier to squirt them down than to try to wash their hands and faces."

Lindy laughed at the visual image of Susan holding the boys while Jeff brought around the garden hose.

Rush's friend strolled to his wife's side and slipped his arm around her slim waist. Susan was a full head shorter than her husband and fit neatly into his embrace. "Are you ready for me to put the steaks on the grill?"

Susan nodded and leaned her supple form against her husband. She went up on tiptoe and brushed a kiss over his cheek. She paused then and smiled up at him. "Anytime you want."

Lindy watched, fascinated by the tender exchange between husband and wife. From what little Susan had told her she knew the couple had gotten off to a rocky start. They'd worked hard to find happiness together and it showed. Jeff and Susan didn't require words to communicate. A shared look, a soft sigh would often be all that was required. How Lindy envied them. How she wished everything was settled between her and Rush. But it wasn't. And he'd be leaving her in just a few, intolerably short days.

*   *   *

They caught the nine o'clock ferry back to Seattle. Jeff dropped them off at the terminal and after Susan and Lindy had shared hugs and Lindy had kissed the boys goodbye, Lindy and Rush walked onto the waiting boat.

Although he shouldn't have been, Rush was astonished at the way Lindy and Susan had become such fast friends. The two had talked and laughed as if they'd known each other since childhood. Now that he thought about it, the two women were quite a bit alike. Both were intelligent, sensitive and personable. And both were in love with navy men. It took a special breed of woman to fit into the military life-style, to accept the long separations, brief reunions and the fact that family must always come second in their husbands' lives.

Both Lindy and he had come away from the evening refreshed. Jeff had given definition to the unknown emotions Rush had been dealing with the past two days. Rush had asked his friend how he managed to leave Susan and the twins and not look back—and had witnessed the instant flash of regret that shot into his friend's eyes. Jeff had explained that the last days before he sailed were always the worst. He didn't want to leave Susan, didn't want to think of not being able to love her for months on end. Nor did he like to think about all that he was missing in his children's lives. He'd been at sea when their first teeth had come in, and on sea trials when they'd taken their first steps. Now he'd be leaving them again, and his mind was crowded with everything he wasn't going to be there to experience.

Then Jeff had asked Rush if he'd had a fight with Lindy recently. Rush's astonishment must have shown because Jeff had laughed and said the same thing happened to him and Susan every time he found out when he'd be sailing. Like clockwork. His fault, usually. But he and Susan had made a promise to each other long ago. No matter what they fought about, they never left anything unsettled between them.

"I'm going to stand outside," Lindy said, cutting into Rush's thoughts. The ferry had been underway for about twenty minutes. She stood and buttoned her sweater before heading for the weather deck.

"Sure. Go ahead," Rush answered. He didn't mind the long ride to and from the shipyard each day. Most of the navy personnel lived in Kitsap County, across Puget Sound from Seattle. But Rush preferred the cultural advantages of living in a big city.

Rush watched as Lindy moved outside the passenger area and stood against the stern, her hands on the rail. The wind whipped the hair from her face and plastered her thin sweater against her soft curves.

Just watching Lindy, Rush felt his heart constrict.

When she'd been holding Timmy and Tommy, laughing with them, bouncing the twins on her hips, Rush hadn't been able to tear his gaze away from her. The earth could have opened up and swallowed him whole and he swore he wouldn't have been aware of it.

Seeing her with those two babies had been the most powerful, most emotional moment of his life. The sudden overwhelming physical desire for her was like a knife slicing into his skin and scraping against a bone—it had gone that deep. Not once, not even with Cheryl had he thought about children. He enjoyed Jeff's sons. They were cute little rascals, but seeing Lindy with those babies had created a need so strong in him he doubted that his life would ever be the same again. He wanted a child. Son or daughter, he didn't care. What did matter was that Lindy be their mother.

Even now, hours later, his eyes couldn't get enough of her as she stood, braced against the wind. He thought about her belly swollen with his seed, her breasts full and heavy, and the desire that stabbed through him was like hot needles. The sensation curled into a tight ball in the center of his abdomen. He'd longed for her physically before now. The thought of making love to her had dominated his thoughts from the first morning he'd stumbled upon her in the bathroom wearing those sexy see-through baby-doll pajamas.

But the physical desire he was experiencing now far exceeded anything he'd previously known. And it was different in ways he couldn't even begin to explain.

Unable to stay parted from her a minute longer, Rush left his seat and stepped outside, joining her at the railing.

Wordlessly he slipped his arm over her shoulder. Lindy looked up at him, and her eyes were unusually dark and solemn. The effort it cost her to smile was revealed in the feeble movement of her mouth.

"Lindy?"

She pressed her index finger across his lips the way she did when she didn't want there to be questions between them. Although she strove valiantly to prevent them, tears filled her sweet, adoring gaze. Inhaling a wobbly breath, she pressed her forehead against his chest in a vain attempt to compose herself.

Rush wrapped his arms around her, needing to comfort her, feeling strangely lost as to what to say or do, and not completely understanding what was wrong. Her lithe frame molded against him and he reveled in the feel of her softness pressed to him. "Honey, what is it?"

She shook her head. "Susan said…"

"She offend you?" Rush couldn't imagine it, and yet the anger rose in him instantly.

Lindy swiftly jerked her head from side to side.

"No...no, of course not." Her arms were around his middle now, her eyes as dry as she could make them. But her chin quivered with the effort.

She lifted a hand and touched the side of his face, her eyes full of such tenderness that it was all Rush could do to meet her gaze.

"Do you remember the night we met?"

He grinned. "I'm not likely to forget it. I nearly tossed you into the street."

"You were perfectly horrible. So uncompromising...so unreadable."

"So arrogant," he added, regretting every harsh word he'd ever said to her.

The corner of her mouth quirked with a swift smile. "A good dose of healthy arrogance to put me in my place as I recall."

He brushed the hair from her face and nodded, resisting kissing her, although it was difficult.

"I disliked you so much.... I actually looked forward to thwarting you. I could hardly wait for you to leave. And now...now I dread it. I wish I could be more like Susan. She's so brave."

"She's had far more experience at this than you." Rush searched her face, and under his scrutiny the normally cool, composed features began to quiver with unspoken anguish. He understood then. She was afraid, almost desperately so, and bravely holding it all inside. Pierced to the quick by his own thoughtlessness, he tightened his grip on her and breathed in the sweet flowery fragrance of her silky dark hair.

"Honey, nothing's going to happen to me."

"But…the gunboats…the missiles."

"I'm coming back to you, Lindy."

She brushed her hands down her cheeks to wipe away the sheen of tears. "You think I'm being silly and emotional, don't you? This isn't wartime, and nothing is likely to happen, but I can't help thinking…"

He took her by the shoulders then, gripping her tightly. "No," he said sternly, his heart filling with a mixture of concern, tenderness and understanding. His mind groped for the words to comfort her. "You're not overreacting. It is going to be dangerous; I'm not trying to whitewash our assignment. But, Lindy, my sweet Lindy, I've never had anything more to live for than I do right this minute."

"You'd better come back to me, Rush Callaghan." She said it as though it were a fierce threat and the consequences would be dire if he didn't.

Death was the only thing that would keep him from Lindy. Unless… The thought was as crippling to him as the fear of him dying was to Lindy. "Then you'd better be waiting for me."

Her sturdy gaze held his and his hands slid from their grip on her shoulder to stroke her slim, swan-like neck.

"You still don't trust my love, do you?" she asked, looking sad and disappointed.

"Yes," he answered, nodding his head for emphasis. "I believe you." He wasn't sure he should—she was so young, so susceptible—but God help him, he needed everything Lindy was so generously offering him.

He took her hand and brushed his lips over her palm and then, because he couldn't resist and didn't give a tinker's damn who was watching, he kissed her mouth.

It was ten by the time the *Yakima* docked in Seattle. The hike to the apartment was a steep climb, but the night was so gorgeous that Lindy didn't want to hurry home. Every minute left was precious and wasting even a single one would be a crime.

"Let's go to the park," she suggested.

Rush looked bewildered for a moment, and asked, "What park?"

"The one here on the waterfront."

"Whatever for?"

Lindy laughed and slapped her hand noisily against her side. "So much for romance."

"Romance?"

"Come on, Rush. I'm finished crying. When you sail off into the sunset, I'll be there wearing a smile. All I ask is for you to humor me a little before you go. If that means taking a short detour to look at the stars from Waterfront Park, I think you should at least be willing.''

''Lindy—'' he said her name on the tail end of a sigh ''—you've got to get up and go to work in the morning.''

She thought for a moment he might refuse her, but he didn't. He slipped his arm around her waist and guided her in the direction of the park.

They climbed the stairs to the second level and stood at the railing, overlooking the quiet green water. The lights from Harbor Island and West Seattle flickered like moonbeams dancing in the distance.

Lindy folded her hands over the cold steel rail, Rush behind her, his chin resting on the crown of her head. ''Remember the last time we were here?'' Lindy asked, thinking of their wild race up the stairs and the joy she'd experienced in having bested him.

''Yes.'' Rush's low voice carried a frown.

Lindy twisted around and gazed up at him. ''Why do you say it like that?''

''You called me Paul. Remember?''

It took her a second to recall that and all that had happened afterward. ''Was that really such a short time ago?'' It felt like years instead of just a few weeks.

''Yes.'' His brow pleated with a grim look.

''No wonder you think I can't possibly know my own heart,'' she whispered, a little desperately. ''No wonder you've never told me how you feel.''

His brows lowered even more, shadowing his face as though he'd realized he'd never said it. "I love you, Lindy."

She closed her eyes and let the words rain down over her heart like velvety smooth flower petals, relishing each one, holding them close so she would have them later when she needed them. "I know," she whispered, the tears back in her voice. "I just wanted to hear you say it one time before you left."

Chapter 9

"Lindy?" Rush dropped his hands from her shoulders. His mind was buzzing, as active as any hive. He felt weak from her touch, weak from the effect of her tears, weak with a desperate need to hold her and make her his own. He'd loved unwisely before, and had given up the dream of ever finding happiness again. And then Lindy, his sweet beautiful Lindy, had slammed into his life, and Rush knew he would never be the same again. His heart felt as if it would burst as he pulled her closer, breathing in the perfumed scent that was hers alone.

"Yes?"

Rush couldn't believe the thoughts that were bouncing around in his mind like Mexican jumping beans. Nothing seemed to keep them still. He loved Lindy. He desired her in a way that went miles beyond the physical. Her courage, her honesty, her spirit—each had shattered every defense he'd managed to erect over the years. From the moment they'd met, she'd played havoc with his heart.

"Rush?" She was staring up at him with wide, inquiring eyes.

"I think we should get married." There. It was out. He watched as the surprise worked its way over her features, touching her eyes first, narrowing them as though she wasn't sure she'd heard him right. Then the excitement and happiness broke out and glowed from every part of her, followed almost immediately by swift tears that brimmed in her clear, brown eyes. When her teeth bit into her lower lip, Rush wasn't sure what to think. She tossed her arms around him, and Rush felt the shiver work through her despite the warmth of the June evening.

"Yes, I'll marry you." Her answer was issued in a small voice that pitched and faltered like a boat bobbing in a storm at sea. "When?"

"We'll buy the ring tomorrow."

She nodded, her eyes bright and eager. "I'll arrange to take off early enough so we can get to the courthouse before it closes."

"The courthouse?"

"For the license." She cast him a stern look that convinced him she would make a wonderful mother.

Once he understood the implication, Rush frowned, unsure how to proceed. "But I don't want to get married *now*."

The happiness that had been shining from her face faded, then vanished completely to be replaced by a stunned, hurt look.

"I see," she whispered, and took a step back, away from him. "You want us to wait six months until you return from this tour?"

It made a hell of a lot of sense to Rush, and when he spoke his voice was soft yet inexorable. "Of course."

"I see."

"Would you quit saying that like I'd just suggested we live in sin?"

Rush could tell that she was struggling to compose her thoughts. Confusion and another emotion he couldn't define tightened her brow, and she looked to be on the verge of breaking into tears—but these weren't tears of sudden happiness.

"I need to think," she announced, stiffly turning away from him and hurrying down the concrete stairs.

Rush, watching her run away from him like a frightened doe, held up his hands in a gesture of utter bewilderment. They couldn't get married so soon. For God's sake, they'd known each other less than three weeks.

* * *

Lindy walked as fast as her legs would carry her, and her heart was pounding so hard she could feel it all the way to her toes. She was a little embarrassed, because she'd assumed that Rush meant for them to marry right away, and she was troubled, too. She didn't want to wait, and she couldn't think of a way of explaining to Rush all the strong and conflicting emotions that were churning inside her.

Within a matter of seconds, Rush's quick-paced steps joined hers.

"For God's sake will you tell me what you find so damn insulting?" he demanded.

Lindy stopped and looked up at him, loving him so much her heart threatened to burst. His eyes seemed unusually dark and, as always, unreadable as he buried his thoughts and his pain deep within himself.

"Insulting? Oh Rush," she whispered contritely, "never that."

"Then why did you take off like a bat out of hell?"

She dropped her gaze to the sidewalk. "I don't want to wait.... When you leave Saturday I want to be..."

"Lindy, that's crazy."

"...your wife," she finished.

Rush's jaw clamped shut, and Lindy saw the muscles in his lean cheek jerk as a hodgepodge of doubts clouded his mind. She didn't blame him, but if he was willing to make a commitment to her now, it seemed fruitless to wait six months.

"I've been through one long engagement," she whispered fiercely. "I have no desire for another. I'll marry you, Rush, and consider myself the luckiest woman alive. But when you place a ring on my finger there will be two, not one."

"Do you realize how ridiculous you sound?"

She watched him intently, her eyes riveted to his. "Yes, I suppose I do, from your point of view."

"In other words, it's all or nothing?"

"No," she answered softly. "I'd marry you tonight if I could, or six months from now if that's what you choose. But if you love me enough to want me as your wife then why should we wait? That's what I don't understand."

His eyes hardened. "But you might regret..."

"No," she cut in, shaking her head so hard her hair whipped across her face. "I swear to you I'm not going to regret it."

Rush inhaled and cast an imploring look to the dark sky as though seeking guidance, and if not that, then divine intervention.

"I don't even want to discuss it."

"Fine," Lindy said with a sigh.

The remainder of the walk was completed in silence. When Rush unlocked the apartment door, Lindy stepped inside, intent on going to her bedroom to give them both space and time to think matters through.

Rush's hand reached for hers, stopping her before she'd gone more than a few steps.

Surprised, she glanced up at him, the light so dim she could barely make out his features.

"It's not right to hurry this when we've only begun to know each other," he said in a tone that was low, husky and deliberately expressionless.

Gently Lindy brushed her fingertips across the taut line of his jaw. "I'm not going to repent at leisure, if that's what you're worrying about. You seem to find it so important that we wait, so we will. But I love you enough right now. I don't have a single doubt that our marrying is the right thing, and nothing is going to change my mind."

"Lindy, it's crazy."

"Marry me now, Rush."

He shook his head. "Six months is soon enough. You need…"

"Me? You're the one who seems to be having all the doubts."

"I'll marry you in six months, Lindy," he said sternly.

Maybe, her mind tossed back. Maybe he would.

Rush studied her for a full minute. "I want you to wear my engagement ring.

The ring finger on her left hand remained dented from the year in which she'd worn Paul's diamond.

Unconsciously she rubbed her thumb back and forth over the groove now, reliving anew the desolation that engagement had brought her. The emotion rippled in her chest, each wave growing broader in its scope. She didn't want to be Rush's fiancée—she'd been Paul's for so long. She'd lost Paul and she could lose Rush, too, in a hundred different ways.

"Will you?" he asked, his voice as unemotional as if he were requesting the time.

Once more Lindy would be forced to face the truth. Rush loved her enough to want a commitment from her but not enough to make her his wife. She would be a fiancée. Again. But not a wife.

A strange light flared in his eyes that she faintly saw in the darkness. "It's important to me."

She sucked in a deep breath and felt all the resistance inside her collapse. Gone was her pride; gone was her conviction; gone was her stubbornness. He wanted to wait. She would. He wanted her to wear his ring. She would do that, too.

"Yes," she whispered brokenly. He needed that assurance. It was Lindy who required more.

Hours later something woke Lindy. Unsure what had stirred her from slumber, she rolled onto her side and rubbed the sleep from her eyes. Across the room a shadow moved and she noted Rush's profile outlined in the doorway of her bedroom. He was leaning against the frame of her door, his head dropped as if he were caught in the throes of some terrible quandary. Something about him, about the way his shoulders slouched and his head drooped, told her this was the last place in the world he wanted to be...or the first.

"Rush, what is it?" She raised herself up on one elbow.

Her words seemed to catch him unawares, and he jerked his head up and straightened. Moving to her side, he sank to the edge of the mattress. Tenderly he brushed the unruly hair from her forehead, his face so intense it seemed knotted. He didn't speak, and Lindy had no way of knowing his thoughts. He groaned then, and his mouth claimed hers in a fiery kiss that threatened to turn her blood to steam. He lifted his mouth from hers and tucked her head beneath his chin, rubbing his jaw back and forth over her crown as if to soak in her softness.

Lindy dragged in a shuddering breath, her senses fired to life by his touch. She'd assumed when she first woke that he wanted to make love to her, but that wasn't his intention. No lover would hold a look of such torment. His eyes were fierce, savage and yet unimaginably tender.

He studied her, and his warm hands stroked her face as though to memorize each loving feature. The smile that touched the edge of his mouth was fleeting. And still he didn't speak. His thumb lightly brushed over her lips, and he closed his eyes briefly as if to compose his troubled thoughts.

"I love you, Lindy," he whispered, in a voice that was at once gruff and soft. "I love you so much it scares the hell out of me."

His arms went around her, holding her as close as he could with the blankets bunched between them. Inhaling a deep breath, he buried his face in her neck.

Lindy's fingers riffled through his dark hair and she lowered her lashes, cherishing this moment, although she wasn't sure she understood it.

"Tomorrow," he told her. "I want you to take off early. We have an appointment at the courthouse."

The longest—and shortest—days of Lindy's life were the three they were required to wait before their wedding. Rush made the arrangements with a navy chaplain, and Jeff and Susan Dwyer stood up for them. The ceremony itself lasted only a few short minutes. Rush stood close at Lindy's side, and she couldn't ever remember him looking more handsome than in full-dress uniform. When he repeated his vows, his voice was strong and confident. Lindy's own was much softer, but equally fervent.

Afterward they went to an expensive restaurant for dinner and were met by several other couples, all navy people, all friends of Rush's. Names and faces flew past Lindy, and after a while she gave up trying to keep track of who was who. She managed to smile at each one and made the effort to thank them for coming to share this day with her and Rush.

Once they were seated, Lindy placed the bouquet of baby's breath and pink rosebuds in her lap. Susan sat on her left and Rush on her right. Rush was talking to Jeff who sat on the opposite side from him. Rush's fingers closed around Lindy's and communicated his frustration at being trapped with all these people when he wanted to be alone with her. Lindy felt the same way. Rush was her husband and she was dying with the need to be his wife in every way. They had such little time left together. Three days and two nights to last them half a year.

"Do you think we're both crazy?" Lindy leaned over and whispered to Susan. There'd been so little time to talk before the ceremony.

"I think it's the most wildly romantic thing I've seen in years." Her new friend's eyes sparkled with shared joy. "A blind man could see how much Rush loves you."

"I honestly didn't think he'd do it," Lindy confessed.

"What? Marry you?"

"Yes, before he left anyway. He wanted to wait until he returned in December, and…then he didn't. I hardly had time to think once he made up his mind.

The past three days have zoomed by. I feel as if I've been on a spaceship—everything's a blur. We've been up every night past midnight discussing the arrangements.

"Didn't you have to work?"

Lindy nodded and suppressed a yawn. "I didn't dare ask for any days off since I've been working such a short time. I regret that now, because I think my supervisor would have understood. But Rush didn't want me to jeopardize my job."

"You'll need it once he's gone," Susan said with a wisdom that must have come from her years as a navy wife. "It's important for you to keep busy. Rush knows that. Having a job to go to every day will help the time he's gone pass all the more quickly. The transition from being together almost constantly to being alone will be smoother, too."

"What about you?" Lindy knew that Susan didn't work outside the home. Her friend couldn't with Timmy and Tommy still so young.

"I manage to do some volunteer work with some of the other navy wives," Susan explained. "We help each other. Once everything settles down, I'll introduce you around."

Lindy smiled, more than willing to meet the others and make new friends. She wanted to do everything that was right to be a good wife to Rush. There was so much to learn, so much to remember. Susan was already a valuable friend, and now she was willing to show Lindy the ropes.

When they left the restaurant, several couples stood outside waiting, and Lindy and Rush were bombarded with flying rice.

Rush had chosen a hotel close to the restaurant for their wedding night. He'd checked in before the ceremony and had their luggage delivered to the suite.

"I didn't think I was ever going to get you alone, Mrs. Callaghan," he whispered to her in the elevator, wrapping his arms around her waist and looking very much as though he wanted to kiss her.

"And exactly what are you planning to do once you have me all to yourself?"

"Oh Lord, Lindy." He breathed in a giant whoosh of oxygen. "You have no idea how hard it's been to keep my hands off you these past few days."

"Yes, I do," she answered softly, blushing just a little. "Because it's been equally difficult for me."

The elevator came to a smooth halt and the door glided cheerfully open. With Rush's hand at her waist guiding her, they walked down the long narrow hallway to the honeymoon suite.

When they reached the room, Rush gently scooped her up and into his arms, managing to hold onto her, juggle the keys and unlock the door.

Rush carried her into the room, slammed the door

closed with his foot and gently laid Lindy upon the huge king-size mattress.

Lindy's arms curled and locked around his neck and, unable to wait a minute longer, she smiled up at him, raised her head and kissed him. Rush groaned and pressed her deeper into the pillows, covering her upper body with his own. Her breasts felt the urgent pressure of his chest, her nipples already tingling with the need to experience his touch. The hammering rhythm of his heart echoed hers and seemed to thunder in her ears. Lindy had waited so long for this night.

Poised above her as he was, Rush's mouth dipped to capture hers.

"I can't believe we're finally here," he whispered, his mouth scant inches above hers.

"I can't believe we're actually married."

"Believe it, Lindy." The moist tip of his tongue outlined her bottom lip.

"I'm going to be a good wife to you," she whispered fervently, planting her hands on either side of his face and guiding his mouth to hers, taking his tongue in her mouth. "You won't regret marrying me.... I promise."

"I have no regrets. Dear God, Lindy, how could I?" Again and again his mouth claimed her until she lost count.

"Lindy, Lindy," he whispered against her neck. "I don't think I can wait much longer.... I wanted

to do this slow and easy, but already I feel like I'm
going to explode, I want you so much.''

They kissed again tempestuously, their mouths
grinding hard, their tongues meeting. The kissing
sparked the coals of their desire with an urgency that
left Lindy trembling in its wake.

Reluctantly, his breath coming in uneven gasps,
Rush moved away from her enough to start unbut-
toning his jacket. Lindy noted that his movements
were abrupt, impatient.

With trembling, uncooperative fingers, she
reached for the zipper at the back of her gown, letting the satin and lace knee-length dress fall to the
floor.

She was about to slip the pale pink camisole over
her head when Rush stopped her.

''Let me,'' he murmured, his eyes consuming her
with a need he couldn't disguise.

She nodded and let her hands fall slack at her
sides.

He stood before her—so tall, so solemn, so intent.
Lindy could feel the spiraling desire wrap itself
around them both, binding them to each other as
effectively as any cord. His hands reached for the
garment's hem and she raised her arms to better aid
him. The silky material whispered against her skin
as he drew it over her torso, and Lindy heard Rush's
soft gasp as her breasts sprang free.

To her surprise, his hands came up to caress her

neck and not her breasts. His touch was unbelievably light, as though he feared the slender thread of
his control would snap. His hands gently stroked the
sloping curve of her neck and then traveled down to
her shoulders, his fingertips grazing her soft, smooth
skin. Lindy's eyes grew heavy under the magic he
wove around her and her body felt warm and rest-
less. The fresh, clean scent of him filled her and her
head rolled to one side. She was caught so completely in the spell he was weaving around her that
she feared she might faint with her need for him.

With the softest of touches his hands found her
breasts, fitting to their underswell, lifting them,
weighing them as though on a delicate balance. The
thumb on each hand grazed an already erect nipple.
Lindy must have moaned or emitted some kind of
sound, because he whispered, "I know, honey, I
know."

Something like a flame began to warm the pit of
her stomach—Lindy could think of no other way to
describe it. The sensation grew more heated and
more intense with every passing flick of his thumbs,
until her nipples became throbbing velvet pebbles
beneath his fingertips. When Lindy was convinced
she could endure no more of this sweet torture, Rush
lowered his mouth to hers. Gently, moistly, he
kissed her lower lip, tugging at it with his teeth.
Then he repeated the process and feasted feverishly
on the upper.

Rush broke away from her long enough to finish undressing, then lowered himself to the mattress, propped beside her and slightly over her. The hand he slipped beneath her back felt cool and smooth against her heated flesh. He used it to arch her toward him, and she gasped when his hot mouth closed over a breast, feasting on one and then the other in turn.

The fire that had started in her stomach spread its flickering flames through her until Lindy felt she was about to be consumed by the heat Rush had generated.

If he didn't take her soon, she was convinced she'd melt with her need. Everything in her seemed to be pulsating. Her breasts throbbed and the apex of her womanhood beat its own pagan rhythm until Lindy tossed her head back and forth, trapped in a delirium of sexual tension.

Rush kissed and caressed her endlessly, his mouth exploring her breasts, her soft belly, her long legs until Lindy thought she'd go mad. Every nerve in her body was shouting with need. Once he had reduced her to quivering helplessness, Rush changed positions so that he was poised directly above her.

His knee parted her thighs and she willingly opened to him. Rush guided himself into position so that the tip of his engorged manhood was pressed against her moist opening.

"Lindy," he whispered hoarsely, "I...love...

you." With each word his pulsating warmth plunged deeper and deeper into her, until he was so far inside her, so firmly locked within her, she was sure he had reached her soul.

Slowly, gradually he began to move, and his swollen heat created the most delicious, most pleasing friction against the most intimate of her surfaces.

Lindy's hands clutched at his broad back, wanting him closer, needing him. She was filled with a tautness, and indescribable demand that became more intolerable with every heart-stopping stroke until she was sure she would scream.

As she struggled to catch her breath, Rush's hands caressed her once more, finding her tingling breasts and then the flat of her stomach.

"Rush...oh Rush...." She tossed her head from side to side, completely lost in the pleasure.

"Kiss me," he pleaded. "Give me your tongue." He put a hand under her head, lifting her mouth to his. Gingerly she explored the hollow of his mouth, running her tongue over his smooth, even teeth. His lower lip was full and when she nipped at it the effect on him was electric. He drove into her again and again, gaining momentum with each thrust until there was only the insistent friction and the sweet, sweet pangs of an all-consuming pleasure. When he climaxed, Lindy felt him throbbing in the innermost recesses of her body and smiled, depleted and utterly content.

Panting, Rush rolled over and pulled her on top of him. He was as breathless as if he'd run for miles, and Lindy's own breathing was as labored as his. Exhausted, she closed her eyes and pressed her flushed face to his heaving chest, allowed herself to be transported, floating in the warm aftermath of his love.

Lindy slept in his arms and Rush watched her, astonished at the woman who was now his wife. Even though he would do nothing to change the deed, he knew deep in his heart that they should have waited before marrying. But he'd wanted her so desperately, and the thought of losing her had been more than he could bear. So he had sealed their future. It was what Lindy wanted—it was what he wanted.

These past weeks with Lindy had begun to fill the emptiness in his soul. His heart had found a home with her. She had wiped away years of cynicism with her smile, erased the bitterness from his memory with her tenderness, healed him and given him a reason to live.

A thin ribbon of sunlight peeked through the crack in the drapes but Rush dared not raise his wrist to check the time for fear of disturbing Lindy's sleep. Lord, what a woman he'd found. Twice more during the night they had made love, and each time she had opened herself to him, holding back noth-

ing. As their bodies had come together, their souls
had merged as well. Their lovemaking was as Rush
had always known it would be. He could hardly bear
the thought of waiting six months to love her again.
And they only had one night more.

"Rush." She tossed his name over her shoulder.
"I've got to push your things aside if I'm going to
get all my stuff into your closet."

"Then do it," he said, delivering another armful
of dresses and blouses to her.

They'd decided to transport her personal things
into Rush's bedroom; she could sleep in his room
when he was away, which only made sense.

"I can't believe you hauled all this to Seattle in
that dinky Rabbit you drive."

"I did."

She was so intent on her task that she didn't notice that Rush had moved behind her. He slipped his
arms around her waist and hugged her, resting his
chin on her shoulder, kissing her neck. Lindy finished pushing the hangers to one side before twisting
around and shyly kissing him back.

"Is that everything?" she questioned, looping her
arms around his neck.

"Just about. You know, there are better ways to
spend a honeymoon."

Her lashes fluttered down. "Yes, I know,

but...but I thought you'd be exhausted by now. I mean...well, you know.''

Rush started unfastening the buttons of her blouse. "I find that you bring out the animal side of my nature.''

Already Lindy could feel her body starting to respond. "You seem to be doing the same thing to me.''

"We've got a million and one things to do,'' he muttered, but his fingers were intent on only one task.

"I know,'' Lindy returned, pulling his shirt free from his waistband.

He stripped the blouse from her shoulders and removed her bra. Her breasts stood out firm and round. He fondled each one, then kissed them in turn. "Did I ever tell you about the morning I walked in on you in the bathroom?''

"Yes,'' she whispered hoarsely.

"I thought at the time your nipples were begging to be kissed.''

"They are now, too.''

Rush groaned. "Oh God, Lindy, I'm never going to get enough of you before I leave.''

"But not for any lack of trying,'' she whispered back, threading her fingers through his hair. Tossing back her head, she whimpered softly as he sucked her breast with the hunger of a starving man. Already his hands were at the snap of her jeans, working that open and then tugging at the zipper. Lindy's fingers were equally busy.

They could hardly make it to the bed fast enough. Wordlessly Rush spread her legs and lowered his body into hers. At his first thrust, Lindy felt an electric charge shoot through her and she cried out.

Their lovemaking was a hungry, wild mating that was both tender and fierce and left them so exhausted they fell into a deep, drained sleep.

A sharp sound broke into Lindy's consciousness, but she resisted waking, not wanting to tear herself away from the warm, lethargic feeling of being held in Rush's arms.

"What the hell?"

Lindy's eyes shot open to discover her brother standing in the doorway of Rush's bedroom. Before she could move or speak, Steve had tossed his seabag on the floor and stormed into the room. With one sweeping motion, he hauled Rush out of bed and slammed him against the wall.

"Just what the hell are you doing in bed with my sister?" he demanded, his fist poised in front of Rush's face.

Chapter 10

"**S**teve!" Lindy screamed. "We're married." She bolted upright and clenched the blankets to her naked breasts with her right hand while holding out her left in proof.

"Married!" Steve exclaimed on a long, slow breath. Gradually he released his grip on Rush's neck. "What the hell! But you hardly know each other. You can't possibly.... You wouldn't."

"It happens that way sometimes," Rush explained, and reached for his pants.

"I don't believe this." Steve shook his head as though the action would dissolve the image before him, then turned and stalked out of the room. He paused at the doorway and looked back. "We need to talk."

Lindy wasn't sure which of them Steve wanted to speak with. What was clear was that Lindy hardly recognized her own brother. His solid, sturdy good looks hadn't changed in the time since she'd last seen him. He was still lean and handsome, the way she'd always remembered him, but his eyes had been so hard, so cruel, as though he would have relished an excuse to fight, even if it was with his best friend.

Rush sat on the edge of the mattress and Lindy moved behind him, looping her arms around his neck. "Are you all right?"

"It's not exactly the way I cherish being woken."

"Me, either." Her teeth nibbled his earlobe, and she rubbed her bare breasts against his back, loving the tingly feeling the action provoked. She grinned with satisfaction as she felt Rush's shoulders tighten and knew he'd experienced the same kind of delicious pleasure.

"Lindy, for God's sake, stop. I've got to go out there and talk to your brother."

The regret in his voice was enough to raise her blood pressure and she sighed, wishing her brother had chosen another time and day to make his appearance.

"I'm coming with you," Lindy said when Rush had finished buttoning his shirt.

"Honey, listen," Rush said, his voice low and

thoughtful. "I think it might be better if Steve and I had a few minutes alone first."

"Why?"

"I want to tell Steve how things went between us," Rush explained. "If he's going to be angry, then I'd rather he was upset with me."

"Hey, Rush, come on. We're in this together." She reached for her clothes and was dressing as quickly as her fingers would allow. "It isn't as if you seduced me, you know. In fact it was more the other way around. You've been a perfect gentleman from the minute we met.... Well, other than that first night—but that's understandable when you think about it.... I think we should both talk to Steve. He is my brother and..."

Rush moved around to her side of the bed and stood in front of her.

Lindy was prepared to argue with her husband if he was determined to be obstinate, but when she glanced up his eyes were filled with such love and tenderness that all her determination to stand at his side and face her brother evaporated.

"Ten minutes," he said, taking her by the shoulders. "That's all I ask."

Denying Rush anything in that moment would have been impossible, and she nodded.

Her husband-of-a-day rewarded her with a quick but infinitely thorough kiss, his tongue darting into her mouth and shooting ripples of pleasure down the

full length of her body. When he released her Lindy
sank back onto the corner of the bed, her legs too
weak to support her.

Rush left the bedroom and closed the door. Lindy
stared at it helplessly, unable to move. Almost immediately the raised, angry voice of her brother followed as he demanded to know what the hell Rush
thought he was doing marrying his little sister.
Lindy didn't hear her husband's reply, but whatever
he said apparently didn't appease Steve, because
shortly afterward Steve started in again. Lindy grimaced at some of the language, impatient to speak
to her brother herself. She was an adult and certainly
capable of choosing her own husband.

She gave Rush the ten minutes she'd promised,
but it was difficult. As the endless seconds ticked
past, Lindy tried to remember the last time she'd
seen Steve. Before he'd divorced Carol, Lindy realized. That was what?—one and a half years ago
now. Steve had been happy then, excited, full of life.
Could it really have been only eighteen months ago?
She hardly recognized Steve as the same man. He
looked so much older than his thirty-three years, and
she wondered if the divorce was responsible for the
changes in him. From what her parents had told her,
Steve and Carol had broken up shortly after their
visit to Minneapolis, and the divorce had been final
for over a year. No one knew any of the details.
Steve hadn't explained a thing, and Lindy hadn't

asked. What went on between her brother and Carol was their business, not hers.

When Lindy couldn't stand it any longer, she stood and walked out of the bedroom. Both men stopped and turned around to face her. Anger flashed from their eyes, and it looked as if they were about to resort to physical violence. Lindy knew she'd timed her entrance perfectly.

"It's good to see you again, Steve," she said with a soft smile, walking to her husband's side and slipping her arm around his waist.

Her brother grumbled something in reply.

"Aren't you going to congratulate Rush and me?"

Steve's eyes hardened as they clashed with Rush's. "I'm not sure."

"Why not?" Lindy feigned a calmness she was far from feeling and smiled up at Rush, letting her warm gaze speak for her.

"Lindy, just what in the hell do you think you're doing?" Steve demanded, looking more upset by the minute. "You've been in Seattle how long? Three, four weeks?"

"Are you saying Rush will make me a terrible husband and that I've made a dreadful mistake? Obviously you know something about him that I don't."

"That's not what I mean and you know it," Steve shouted. He paused long enough to rake his fingers through his hair, mussing the well-groomed effect. "What about Paul Abrams?"

Lindy met her brother's gaze without emotion. "What about him?"

"You loved him...or so you said. Hell, the last time I heard from you, your heart was broken and you didn't know if you wanted to go on living. Remember?"

"Of course I remember."

"And that's all changed?" His voice carried a harsh sound of reprimand. "It didn't take you very long to forget him, did it? So much for undying love and devotion. Well, little sister, did you ever stop to think what could follow next? If your affections can change overnight, what's going to happen when Rush has sea duty? Are you going to divorce him once he's out of sight because you find yourself attracted to another man?"

Lindy felt her husband tense at her side. She wasn't pleased with Steve's insinuation, either, but she was willing to let it pass. "As you recall, Paul was the one who conveniently forgot about me. Thank God he did, otherwise I would never have met Rush."

"You're saying that now. God, what a mess." Steve abruptly turned away and marched to the other side of the room. Just as sharply, he turned back to face them. "Of all the people in the world, I thought you were the one I could trust the most."

His comment was directed at Rush.

"She's just a kid." The look Steve tossed his friend suggested Rush had resorted to robbing a day-care center.

"I'm twenty-two," Lindy cried, piqued.

"Damn it, Lindy. You don't know a thing about marriage."

"She knows enough about being a wife to satisfy me," Rush answered calmly.

"She's too young for you," Steve shouted, and started in again with hardly a breath. "Any fool could see she married you on the rebound. I thought you were smarter than this, Callaghan. You took advantage of her."

"If he'd taken advantage of me," Lindy cut in, growing more impatient with her sibling by the moment, "he wouldn't have married me."

"Of course he married you. He knew I'd beat the hell out of him if he didn't."

From the tight expression her brother wore, Lindy could see that he'd relish the opportunity to fight with Rush.

"Steve, stop it," she pleaded, holding out her hands. "I'm married, and although you seem to think it's some great tragedy, I don't. I plan on being a good wife to Rush. This isn't an overnight fling. We're committed to each other."

"I don't give this so-called marriage three months."

Rush's hands knotted into tight fists, but when he went to step forward, Lindy stopped him. Her husband had done an admirable job of keeping his cool, but Steve's accusations were beginning to wear on them both, and Lindy could tell Rush wouldn't put up with much more.

"Have you told Mom and Dad?"

"Of course. I'm not ashamed of what we've done." But she'd waited until after the ceremony to announce she was married for fear her mother would try to talk her out of it. When she did phone her parents, Grace Kyle hadn't been able to disguise her shock and had started to weep. When her father had come on the line, he'd been equally stunned, almost embarrassed, stumbling over his words, clearly not knowing what to say. It wasn't until Rush had talked to both her parents that Lindy's family had made an effort to offer their congratulations.

Steve's eyes narrowed. "I should kick your teeth down your throat for this, Callaghan."

Rush's mouth quirked into a half smile. "I'd like to see you try."

"Stop it, both of you!" Lindy cried, shocked at both men. "I don't know what's the matter with you, Steve, but this is my honeymoon. I have only one night left to spend with my husband, and I don't intend to waste it arguing with you."

"The *Mitchell* is leaving in the morning?"

Once more Steve's question was directed to Rush as he chose to ignore Lindy.

Rush nodded.

The two men stood not more than ten feet apart and glared heatedly at each other, issuing silent challenges. Steve broke away first, picked up his seabag and headed toward the door.

"I'll leave you two alone."

"It would be appreciated," Rush answered.

Steve turned back to face his friend and Lindy couldn't remember when his dark eyes had been more intense. "You hurt her, Callaghan, and you'll answer to me personally."

The tension in the room was so electric it was a miracle lightning didn't flash from the ceiling. It seemed to arc and flow between the two men, ready to ignite at any moment.

"I thought you knew me better than that," Rush answered through clenched teeth.

"I don't trust anyone. Not anymore. Just remember what I said. If Lindy's ever unhappy, I'm going to hold you responsible."

A throbbing, wounded silence filled the room after the front door slammed. Lindy sat on the davenport and forcefully expelled her breath. "What is his problem?"

"When was the last time you saw your brother?" Rush wanted to know, taking the seat beside her and reaching for her hand.

"About a year and a half ago. Steve and Carol drove to Minneapolis when Steve was on shore leave. They were so much in love and so happy, we were all stunned when a few months later we got a letter that said he'd filed for divorce. We never knew why. I think he would have told me had I asked, but I never did. What happened between him and Carol is their business."

"The divorce changed him," Rush explained softly.

"You're telling me. But his letters were never like this. He was always so encouraging, so upbeat. When he heard what happened with Paul, his letter helped me so much. He understood so well what I was going through, but now I feel like I hardly know him."

"He's upset," Rush answered after a moment. "He'll come around once he has time to think things through. He knows us both, probably better than anyone else."

Lindy nodded. "I'm not fickle and my brother knows that. I didn't marry you on the rebound. I swear that, Rush. I love you."

Rush's face broke into a slow, relaxed grin and he draped his arm over her shoulders. "And I love you, wife."

Lindy tucked her head beneath his chin and snuggled into his warm embrace, cherishing the closeness they shared. She didn't expect anyone else to understand something she couldn't explain herself. Finding Rush was like stumbling upon her other half. With him she was whole.

"What went wrong with Steve and Carol?" Lindy asked quietly as her thoughts drifted back to her brother. She was concerned about the changes she saw in him.

Rush was silent for a long moment. "I'm not sure. Like you, I felt it was his and Carol's business, but I'm almost certain she was unfaithful."

"No way." If Lindy knew anything about her ex-sister-in-law it was that gentle, sweet Carol would never cheat on Steve. "She just isn't the type."

"Then I haven't any idea what went wrong."

"How sad," Lindy murmured. It was obvious to her that Steve had changed drastically since his divorce. Although she couldn't believe Carol had been unfaithful to her brother, that would explain Steve's statement about not trusting anyone anymore.

"I think we could both learn a valuable lesson from what happened with your brother's marriage," Rush said, his voice tightening.

"What?" Lindy asked, and raised her head to study her husband's face. His eyes had darkened slightly and she wasn't able to read his thoughts, but she had a good idea what he was thinking. And she didn't like it. Not one damn bit. "Are you going to start lecturing me, Rush Callaghan?"

"Lecturing you?"

"Yes. I have a fair idea of what you're going to say."

The muscles of his face relaxed into a half smile as he leaned against the back of the davenport and crossed his arms. His knowing eyes came alive with mischief. "Oh, you do, do you?"

"You were about to give me some dopey line about what we're experiencing now being some kind of euphoric stage all lovers go through."

"I was?"

"Yes, you were. You were going to say we're experiencing a time when everything and everyone is perfect. There's no one else on the planet but us and nothing else but our newly discovered love."

Rush's brows arched, but if he was portraying anything other than amusement, Lindy couldn't tell.

"And..."

"There's more?" he asked, and laughed, his rich baritone sounding relaxed and amused.

"Oh, I'm just getting to the good part." She stood and rubbed the palms of her hands together, sorting through her thoughts.

"Well?" he pressed, having trouble disguising his amusement.

"You're about to tell me that the tension is gone. We've stepped over the line, entered the bedroom and now that territory has been charted."

"Not as much as I'd like, but we'll make up for

lost time later.'' Rush's words were more promise than comment.

"Don't interrupt me.''

"Sorry.'' He didn't look the least bit repentant.

"You're going to tell me we're about to step off cloud nine and should expect to be hit with a healthy dose of reality. We could be headed for trouble now. If we aren't careful, what happened to Steve and Carol could happen to us.''

All traces of amusement faded from Rush's eyes and his face tightened. Lindy knew she was right. "By this time tomorrow, you'll be gone.'' She forced herself to offer him a brave smile. "And I'm going to be alone.''

Rush stood. His eyebrows were pulled down into a heavy ledge of concern. "That's right, Lindy. Up until this point everything's gone smoothly for us. Our whole world has been telescoped into a two-part universe. After tomorrow everything will change, and I doubt that it'll ever be exactly the same again. In two weeks you could be wondering how you ever imagined yourself in love with me.''

"That will never happen.'' She shook her head hard for emphasis.

"In two months, you'll have forgotten what I look like.''

From his narrowed, tight expression, Lindy knew he wouldn't listen to any denials. She hadn't started this conversation to argue with him. The last thing she wanted was for them to spend their remaining hours fighting.

"You're married to a man you hardly know who's going to be leaving you for half a year. The next time I see you, it'll be close to Christmas."

She crossed her arms and cleared her throat loudly. "Have you finished?"

"Finished what?"

"Your lecture."

"Lindy, I'm serious. I—"

"You're not saying anything I haven't already thought about a hundred times. I love you, Rush, and I've never been more sure of anything in my life. My feelings aren't going to change in ten days or ten years."

Tenderly he wrapped her in his arms then, and held her close. If there was anything more he wanted to tell her, he left it unsaid.

Hours later Rush lay on his back in bed with Lindy nestled, sleeping, in his arms. He hadn't been able to sleep, dreading the thought of leaving her. Getting married the way they had was possibly the most irresponsible thing he'd done in his life. But he didn't care. Given the same set of circumstances he'd marry Lindy again. Gladly.

She astonished him. She was so sure, so absolutely confident they'd done the right thing. Her unwavering trust had been contagious. God knew, he'd wanted her badly enough. Steve seemed to think he'd taken advantage of her, and perhaps he had, but that couldn't be changed now. Lindy was his wife, and by all that he considered holy, he planned to be a good husband to her.

He closed his eyes and inhaled the fresh scent of jasmine and perfume that was Lindy's alone, knowing full well that within a few hours he would be walking away from her.

Rush thought his heart would burst with the love he felt for his wife. He softly kissed the crown of her head, cradled in the crook between his neck and shoulder.

Lindy Callaghan was some kind of woman. They'd made love together, their bodies moving in perfect synchronization, as though they'd been married for years. All afternoon and evening, they'd teased and played lovers' games, pretending they had forever. But it wasn't enough. Not nearly enough. Rush wanted her again. Now. But he had the feeling making love to her a thousand times wouldn't be enough to satisfy him.

Lindy woke from a sound sleep when Rush pushed the thin fabric of her nightgown aside, his fingers light and quick. She hardly felt his movements until his mouth closed greedily over her nipple. She sucked on her bottom lip to keep from whimpering as the hot stab of pleasure pierced her.

Her head ground into the pillow with every moist stroke of his tongue. And when his teeth gently tugged at the raised peaks of her breasts, it felt as if he were pulling at a thread that was linked to the heart and heat of her womanhood. She moaned anew at a pleasure so intense it was akin to pain, and still Rush sucked at the pebbled hardness. Again and again, like a butterfly flitting from flower to flower, he sampled the sweetness of the nectar from her breasts until he was pleasurably sated.

When she was sure she was about to melt with liquifying, pulsating need, Rush lifted his head. He lay on his side and slid his hand down the smooth length of her stomach until his caressing fingers tangled in the nest of wispy hair. He paused.

Lindy stopped breathing as his fingers slowly delved deeper, charting fresh territory as they sought the opening to the moist warmth. With his probing finger inside her, Lindy lifted her bottom and rotated her hips, saying without words what she wanted. Rush's mouth returned to her nipple and the hot cord of pleasure joining her breasts and the core of her womanhood was drawn even tighter as he connected the two ends.

When he had nearly driven her to the limits of sanity, Rush moved his body over hers. In one unbroken action, he entered her.

They both gasped at the strength of the undiluted pleasure.

Their eyes met and locked in the darkness. He was buried as deeply inside her as he could go, and still he didn't move. Lindy felt his limbs tremble as he struggled to gain control of his raging desire. She moaned in protest and squirmed beneath him, grinding her hips against him until he cried out her name in an agonized plea.

"Honey...please...don't do that."

"I can't help it." Once more she raised her bottom enough to experience the intimate friction she craved so desperately.

"Lindy." He hissed her name again through clenched teeth. "For pity's sake, don't.... Every time you do that...oh, Lindy...."

She gazed up at his tortured face and lifted her head to kiss him. He responded by thrusting his tongue in her mouth while all ten fingers tunneled through her hair.

He started to move then in a long, slow stroke that plunged him deep within her. She whimpered when he withdrew, but he quickly sank into her again and again and again, bringing them to a shared climax several moments later. Together they cried out, their hearts sailed and they soared into a new shining universe as their voices shouted in joyous celebration.

Still sheathed inside her, Rush whispered urgently, "You're mine, Lindy. Mine."

"Yours," she whispered in return. "Only yours."

* * *

Lindy had never seen so many people gathered in one place in her life. It seemed the entire navy had come to watch the tugboats tow the *Mitchell* out of Sinclair Inlet.

Susan Dwyer stood at Lindy's side on the long pier, looking at the huge aircraft carrier as it sliced through the dark green waters. Helicopters from the local television stations hovered overhead and small planes zoomed past to get pictures of the carrier as it was tugged away from the Bremerton shipyard.

"How do you feel?" Susan asked, shouting above the noise of the cheering crowd.

"I don't know." Lindy shook her head, feeling a little numb. A lump rose in her throat. When she'd kissed Rush goodbye, she'd felt the reluctance and tension in him, but no shrinking. As much as he wanted to stay with her, as much as he longed for them to be together, he longed for the sea more. He was going to leave her because it was his duty, his destiny. He belonged to the navy, and she had only been granted second rights.

"I'm not going to cry." That much Lindy knew.

"Good girl." Susan was dry-eyed herself. "You're going to do just fine. We both are. These six months will fly by. Just you wait and see, and before we know it they'll both be back, randy as hell and—" She stopped abruptly and heaved in a deep breath. "Who am I trying to kid? It's going to be the pits.'' Her gaze clouded and she bit into her trembling bottom lip. "I think I'm pregnant again.''

Lindy didn't know what to say. "Does Jeff know?''

"Nope. I went off the Pill last month when they left the first time. There didn't seem to be any reason to keep taking them when Jeff was going away for all those months. I forgot to take the stupid things half the time anyway. Then Jeff was home and I didn't even think about it until yesterday morning.''

"Why then?''

"I threw up.''

"Oh, Susan. Are you going to be all right?''

"If I said yes, would you believe me?''

"Probably.''

Her friend sighed. "Well, don't. I have miserable pregnancies. And I don't think Jeff's going to be pleased, either. We'd agreed to wait at least another couple of years.''

Lindy found a tissue in her purse and handed it to her friend, who quickly wiped the moisture from her pale cheeks.

"Tears are another sure sign with me.''

"I'd better keep track of these symptoms,'' Lindy muttered absently.

Susan paused, blew her nose and turned to face Lindy. "What do you mean?''

"Rush and I weren't using any birth control, either.... It wasn't the right time of the month for me to start the Pill, and well, to be honest, we didn't discuss it.''

"Oh, Lindy, how do we let these things happen?''

Lindy didn't have an answer to that. Not once during the last two nights had she given any thought to the fact that she could become pregnant. It certainly wouldn't be any great tragedy, but she would have preferred to wait a year or two before they started a family. Rush hadn't said a word, either. It seemed improbable that he hadn't thought of the possibility.

"You want to come back to the house with me and share a hot fudge sundae and a jar of pickles?'' Susan asked seriously.

Lindy shook her head. "My brother arrived yesterday. We haven't had much of a chance to talk.''

"Keep in touch.''

"I will,'' Lindy promised.

Steve was watching the newscast that showed the *Mitchell* pulling out of Puget Sound when Lindy entered the apartment. He didn't so much as look away from the television screen when she entered the living room, and Lindy paused, anticipating the worst.

"If you're going to yell at me, do it now and get it over with,'' she said, standing just inside the room. After saying farewell to Rush she didn't need anything more to dampen her already low spirits.

Her brother leaned forward and pressed the remote control dial, turning off the television set.

"Dear God, Lindy, what have you done?"

"I just said goodbye to my husband," she answered him, in a steady, controlled voice.

"Why'd you marry him?"

"For the usual reasons, I assure you."

Steve wiped a hand down his face. "I wish to hell I could say how happy I am for you, but I can't. I know you too well, Lindy. This marriage just isn't going to work. You're not the type of woman who's going to accept the life-style the navy demands. How can you possibly expect to know a man well enough to marry him in three weeks?"

"I know everything I need to."

"I suppose he told you about Cheryl?"

She squared her shoulders and stiffened her spine in a defiant gesture. She knew there'd been someone else, but Rush hadn't filled in the details. She hadn't told him everything about Paul, either.

"Did he?" Steve pressed.

"No," she flared.

"You're married to a man and you know nothing about his past."

"I love Rush and he loves me. That's all I need." Lindy was painfully conscious of her brother's adverse feelings toward her and Rush, but she was at a loss to understand his hostility. Unless his divorce had completely tainted his views on marriage.

Steve shook his head, his face pinched in a deep frown. "I'm afraid you've made the biggest mistake of your life, Lindy Kyle."

She stepped into the room and sat on the sofa arm. "The name's Lindy Callaghan, now."

Chapter 11

Susan Dwyer met Lindy at the front door. "Welcome," she said, bringing her inside the house. A group of women sat in the living room and smiled enthusiastically when Lindy entered the room. She recognized several of the faces from the restaurant where she and Rush had eaten their wedding dinner, but remembering all their names would have been impossible.

"Hello," Lindy said, cordially nodding her head toward the others. She took the only available chair and crossed her long legs, hoping she gave the appearance of being at ease. Susan had invited her over for a late lunch the week before, but her friend hadn't mentioned that anyone else would be present.

"I thought it was time you got to know some of the other wives," Susan said as a means of explanation.

"And if no one else is going to say it, I will," an attractive blonde with wide blue eyes piped up. "We're all anxious to get to know you better."

"We've all been crazy about Rush for years. I'm Mary, by the way."

"I'm Paula," the blonde who'd spoken first added.

"Hello, Mary and Paula." Lindy raised her hand.

Four of the others quickly introduced themselves. Sissy, Elly, Sandy and Joanna.

"Did you get the wives' packet?" Joanna wanted to know scooting to the edge of her seat.

Lindy's eyes shot to Susan. "I don't think so." The *Mitchell* had been gone almost a month now and because Lindy had been so busy with her job and worrying about her brother, she hadn't been able to get together with Susan as soon as she'd wanted.

"I'll take care of that right now." Joanna opened a briefcase and brought out a thick packet. She stood and delivered it to Lindy. "This is a little something the navy hands out to new wives so they aren't completely in the dark about what they've gotten themselves into having married a man in the military."

"A sort of finding-your-sea-legs-while-still-on-land idea," Susan explained.

Lindy opened the packet to find several brochures

and booklets. There was one on the social customs and traditions of the navy—guidelines for the wives of commanding officers and executive officers, another on overseamanship, and several others, including one that gave the history of the U.S. Navy.

"An issue of *Wifeline* should be in there, too."

"Joanna's one of the ombudsmen for the *Mitchell*," Susan explained.

Lindy wasn't sure what that meant. "Oh," she said weakly, hoping she didn't sound completely stupid.

Joanna must have read the confusion in her eyes, because she added. "I act as a liaison between the command and the families. If you have a problem with something, come to me."

"Wonder Woman here will take care of it for you," Sissy commented and smiled at Joanna. "I know she's helped me often enough."

"I'm not completely sure I understand," Lindy admitted, with some reluctance. Although Steve had been in the service fifteen years, as long as Rush, Lindy had little technical understanding of the way the military worked.

"Let me give you an example," Joanna said and tapped her index finger against her lips while she thought. "Let's say you get sick and need to go to the hospital when Rush is on a cruise, and there's some kind of screwup there and they won't take you."

"Call Joanna." Seven voices chimed in unison.

"I see."

Joanna playfully cocked her head and slanted her mouth in a silly grin, which caused the others to laugh. "Mainly my job is to be sure that no one feels they need to face a problem alone. When you married Rush, you married his career, too. You belong to the navy now just as much as Rush does. If you've got a problem there will always be someone here to help."

"That's good to know." Lindy hadn't thought about it before, but what Joanna said made sense. The knowledge that someone was there to lend a helping hand gave her a comforting sense of belonging. Although she knew Susan was her friend, Jeff's wife had been her only contact with Rush's life.

"When the guys are around there aren't that many problems, but once they're deployed we have to stick together and help each other," Sissy added, and a couple of the others nodded their agreement.

"What do you mean there aren't that many problems with the guys around?" Mary, a slim redhead, cried. "I don't suppose anyone happened to mention to Lindy the hassles of shifting responsibilities and..."

"Hey, the poor girl just got married. Let's not hit her over the head with everything just yet."

"No," Lindy interrupted. "I want to know."

"It's just that we—meaning we wives—are left to handle the domestic situations when the men are at sea. It's not as if we have a whole lot of choice in the matter. Someone's got to do it. But then once our husbands sail home we're supposed to return to the docile role of wife and mother and automatically let the men take over. Sometimes it doesn't work that well."

"I don't imagine it would," Lindy said thoughtfully, and sighed inwardly. Briefly she wondered what problems the years held in store for her and Rush. She'd never thought about the shifting roles they'd need to play in their family life. It was a little intimidating, but she'd only been a bride for a month and didn't want to anticipate trouble.

"Every time Chuck's due back home, I get sick," Mary confessed, looking disgusted with herself. "It's all part of the syndrome."

"The homecoming is wonderful, but Wade and I tiptoe around each other for days for fear of saying or doing something that will ruin our reunion," another wife explained.

"We choose to ignore the obvious problems and pass over strife until it's time for him to be deployed again."

"That's when it really hits the fan," Susan inserted.

"What do you mean?" Lindy was curious to know. She could understand what the others were saying, although she hadn't been married long enough to experience with Rush a lot of what the women were warning her about. But the time would come when she was bound to, and she was eager to recognize the signs.

"It seems we're all susceptible to arguing before our husbands' leave," Joanna explained.

Lindy remembered how Rush had purposely picked a fight with her the afternoon he'd learned the repairs to the *Mitchell* had been completed.

"Rush jumped all over me for putting his book away," Lindy told the others. "I didn't understand it at the time. It was so ridiculous, so unreasonable and not like him at all."

The others nodded knowingly.

"I imagine it was about that time that Rush realized he loved you," Susan added smoothly. "Jeff pulled the same thing. He always does. The day he comes home and suggests it's time I go on a diet, I know what's coming. He's just learned when he'll be deployed. Jeff loves what he does, but he loves me and the kids, too. It's a crazy kind of tug-of-war that goes on inside him. He dreads leaving, hates the thought of all those months apart, and at the same time he's eager to sail. He can hardly wait to get out on the open seas."

"Try to make sense out of that if you can," Mary grumbled. "But this is all part of being a navy wife."

"And then there's the constant knowledge that we can be transferred at any time."

"Say, did anyone else hear the rumor that the *Mitchell* could be reassigned to Norfolk?"

"It's just gossip, Sissy," Joanna answered. "There's no need to worry about it now."

"See what I mean," Susan told Lindy with a soft laugh.

"You mean the *Mitchell* might transfer its home port to Norfolk?" Already Lindy was thinking about what would happen with her job if Rush was to be stationed in another state. She'd have to go with him and leave Seattle. Of course she could always find another job, but she didn't relish the thought. A growing knot of concern started to form in her stomach.

"The *Nimitz* was transferred from Norfolk to Bremerton," Sissy reminded the group.

"Two joys of navy life," Mary muttered disparagingly. "Deployment separation and cross-country moves."

"If worse comes to worst, we'll survive."

It was apparent to Lindy that Joanna was the cool voice of reason in this friendly group. Lindy still had trouble keeping track of who was who, but felt that she was going to fit in nicely. It was as though she were being welcomed into a sorority. The other navy wives' acceptance of her was automatic, their reception warm.

"We always survive," Susan added softly. "Now, as I said earlier, we're not going to knock poor Lindy over the head with everything in one afternoon."

"Yeah, we plan to give it to you in small doses."

"Has anyone else stopped to figure out how much time married couples are separated if the husband is in the navy?" Mary asked, holding a calculator in her hand. Her fingers were punching in a long list of numbers that she called out at regular intervals. "According to my figures, during a twenty-year enlistment—" her fingers flew over the keys "—the husband and wife will spend six years apart."

"Six years?" Lindy repeated while the numbers whirled around her head.

"It's not so bad," Susan said, and patted Lindy's hand to tell her she understood her friend's distress. "In small doses."

"While I've got everyone here," Joanna added, snapping her briefcase shut and setting it aside. "Remember you need to have your letters mailed by the fifteenth of each month."

The other women nodded, apparently already aware of the deadline. Susan had explained to Lindy earlier that because the *Mitchell* was deployed in unfriendly waters, the mail would be flown in with supplies only once a month.

"When are we going to eat?" Sissy asked, craning her neck to peek into the kitchen.

"Every time Bill's gone, Sissy gains ten pounds."

"I work it off once he's home, so quit teasing me."

"I could make a comment here, but I won't," Sandy muttered, and the others laughed.

"Well, if a certain someone doesn't feed me soon, I'm going to fade away before your very eyes." Dramatically Sissy placed the back of her hand against her forehead and released a long, expressive sigh.

"Okay, okay," Susan said with a laugh. "Lunch is served."

Everyone stood at once and moved into the kitchen. The table was arranged with a variety of salads, buffet style. Plates and napkins were arranged at one end and the forks fanned out attractively.

"I brought the recipe for the Cobb salad, in case anyone's interested," Paula commented.

"I wish you had said something," Lindy complained under her breath to Susan. "I could easily have brought something."

"You're our guest of honor."

"We're all dying to know how you met Rush," Sissy said and Joanna moved Lindy to the front of the line and handed her a plate.

"I think he's sexy as hell, and Doug told me he

could hardly believe Rush would marry someone he only knew two weeks."

"Well, actually," Lindy murmured as an embarrassed flash of color entered her cheeks, "it was closer to three weeks."

The women laughed.

Sissy pressed her hand over her heart and sighed. "That's the most romantic thing I've heard in years and years."

Elly's shoulders moved up and down as well in an elongated sigh. "I always knew when the big man tumbled, he'd fall hard."

"He's so handsome," Mary interjected.

"So dedicated," Paula added.

"Until the night of your wedding dinner, he was always so...detached and distant. We all noticed the change in him."

"Thank you," Lindy answered softly.

"I bet he's a good lover."

"Sissy!"

Lindy laughed because although the others had been quick to chastise their friend they eagerly looked in her direction for a response. Not willing to disappoint them, she wiggled her eyebrows a few times and nodded.

"I knew it. I just knew it," Sissy cried.

"Are we going to eat, or are we going to talk about Lindy's love life all afternoon?" Joanna asked.

The women looked at each other, came to some sort of tacit agreement and set their plates aside.

"Are you all right?" Jeff asked Rush as he moved past his friend to the engine-order telegraph.

"Fine." The word was as sharp as a new razor. Rush wasn't willing to discuss his problems with anyone, not even Jeff.

"There's got to be some logical explanation why Lindy hasn't written."

"Right," Rush answered, but he avoided looking at his friend, doing his best to look busy. He didn't want to be rude, but he wasn't going to discuss his troubles either.

"Susan's letter says the wives' association had Lindy over for lunch recently."

"Is that supposed to reassure me?"

"I think it should." Jeff unfolded Susan's thick letter and scanned its contents. "Lindy's kept in close contact with Susan and the others."

"That doesn't mean a damn thing."

"Apparently they had a wedding shower for her."

That made him feel a whole lot better, Rush mused sarcastically. Lindy seemed to have forgotten she had a husband, but she was busy accepting wedding gifts.

Jeff paused and cleared his throat. "It seems the wives went together and got Lindy a long silk nightie."

Rush didn't respond. His jaw was clenched so tightly that he was convinced his back molars would crack. He'd been four interminable weeks without a single word from Lindy. A whole damn month. The knot in his stomach was tight enough to double him over. His nerves were shot. He found himself snapping at his men, behaving irrationally, becoming angry and taking it out on everyone else. And worse, he wasn't sleeping. For two nights now he hadn't been able to so much as close his eyes. Every time he did, the images that filled his mind were of Lindy with another man, presumably Paul. The hot surges of anger and adrenaline that shot through him were so strong that any chance of falling asleep was a lost cause. Lindy might as well have taken a knife and cut open a vein as not written.

Unwillingly Rush's mind leaped to a memory of how it had been with Cheryl. At first there'd been a flood of letters, filled with all the right phrases, everything a man longs to hear when he's separated from the woman he loves. Then Cheryl's letters had petered out to a handful in a month, and then just a sporadic few before his return.

But damn it all to hell, Lindy was his wife. He'd slipped a diamond ring on her finger and committed his life to her. He'd expected more of her than this. But apparently she took her vows lightly because she'd sure as hell forgotten him the minute he was out of sight.

It was a mistake to have married her. But he'd been so much in love with her that he'd refused to listen to the calm voice of reason. He'd lost one woman and feared losing another. He should have known standing before a preacher wasn't going to make any difference, but he would never have believed Lindy could do this. All her reassurances about knowing her own heart had fooled him. She'd been so positive they were doing the right thing. None of that confidence was worth a damn now. They'd both made a mistake. A bad one. At the rate things were progressing, this marriage could be the single worst disaster of his life.

"I'm going below," Rush announced, walking away from the gyrocompass repeater, which indicated the *Mitchell*'s course. The sight of Jeff holding a letter from home was more than Rush could take. He needed to escape before he said or did something he'd regret.

Jeff nodded, but his brow was creased with tight bands of concern.

Once in his compartment, Rush lay on his back with his hands cupped behind his head. Steve was right. Rush had known it the minute his friend had said as much. Lindy had married him on the rebound, and now that he was gone she'd realized what a terrible error in judgment she'd committed and wanted out.

They'd been living in a fairy tale, forced to share

the apartment the way they were, and like a fool Rush had gotten sucked into the fantasy. Lindy had been wounded by love and Rush had been a convenient source of comfort to her damaged ego.

Now that he was gone, Lindy realized their mistake. The muscles of his stomach knotted when he realized how helpless he was in this situation. Lindy didn't love him.

Now all he had to worry about was if she was pregnant. Not using any protection had been a conscious decision on his part. They hadn't even talked about it the way couples should—hadn't discussed the possibility of starting a family so soon. It wasn't that Rush had been so eager for Lindy to get pregnant, he realized with a flash of insight. But he hadn't wanted a repeat of what had happened with Cheryl. If Lindy's stomach was swollen with a baby when he returned, he didn't want any question in his mind about who was the father.

Rush refused to believe he'd actually done anything so stupid as to play that sort of silly mind game. Lindy wasn't going to cheat on him—he refused to even consider the possibility. But then he'd honestly assumed she loved him, too—the same way he loved her. It hadn't even taken her a month to forget him.

Lindy let herself into the apartment and stopped when she found her brother sitting in front of the television, watching a late afternoon talk show. Steve's behavior was really beginning to concern her. He'd been assigned shore duty, and when he wasn't working he sat around the apartment with a lost, tormented look that reminded her of how she'd felt when she'd first arrived in Seattle. His behavior wasn't the only thing that was getting on her nerves. He'd become so cynical and so sarcastic about life. His thinking seemed so negative that she didn't like to talk to him anymore. There'd been a time when she'd admired him for the way he'd handled the emotional trauma of the divorce, but his letters had been a convenient front. It became clearer every day that the healing process hadn't even started in Steve. He still loved Carol, and he needed to either patch things up between them or accept the divorce as final. Otherwise it was going to ruin his life.

"Hi," she said, and walked into the kitchen, setting down the grocery bag on the counter. "What's Donahue got to say today?"

"Who?"

"The guy whose program you're watching."

"Hell, I don't know. Something about nursing mothers."

"And that interests you?"

"It's better than staring at some stupid game show."

"It's a beautiful day. You should be outside."

"Doing what?"

Lindy sighed. "I don't know. Something. Anything."

Steve stood and came into the kitchen. "Do you want me to do something for dinner? Peel potatoes, that sort of thing?"

She thanked him for his offer with a smile. "I've got everything under control." Opening the refrigerator, she set the milk inside and decided now was as good a time as any to wade into shark-infested waters. "Is Carol still living in Seattle?" Lindy asked the question and then turned to face her brother.

"Carol who?"

His words may have been flippant, but he couldn't disguise the instant flash of pain in his eyes.

"Carol Kyle, your wife."

"Ex-wife," he corrected bitterly. "As far as I know she is."

"I think I'll give her a call."

A year seemed to pass before Steve answered. "Before you start meddling in someone else's troubles, you'd better take care of your own, little sister."

Lindy's heart flew upward and lodged in her throat. "What do you mean by that?"

Steve pointed toward the mail that was stacked on the kitchen table. "You must have put the wrong address on that long letter you've been writing all month to Rush, because it's been returned."

"Oh, no." A sickening feeling invaded her limbs and her eyes widened with dread. "Returned? But why?" She reached for the thick manila envelope and checked the address. "Oh, Steve, what will Rush think if he doesn't get any mail from me?"

"The only thing he can assume under these circumstances. That you married him on the rebound and regret it."

She raised her hands in a gesture of abject defeat. "But I don't feel that way, not at all."

"Lindy, sit down. You look like you're about to faint." Her brother pulled out a chair and carefully lowered her into it. He walked a couple of times around her, as though gathering his thoughts on how to handle the situation.

Tears of frustration were hovering just beneath the surface. She'd faithfully written Rush each night, pouring out her heart to her husband, reassuring him each day how much she loved him and how proud she was to be his wife. She'd written about meeting the other wives and told him about the social get-together they were planning to celebrate the halfway mark of the six-month cruise. She'd drawn a picture of the lacy silk nightie the girls had given her as a wedding gift and told him how eager she was to model it for him.

There were weeks when she'd scribbled long epistles as many as six and seven times. Since the mail was only going to reach him once a month,

Lindy had written it in journal form, marking the days.

To her surprise, this long separation wasn't anything like he'd suggested it would be. Rush had warned her that two weeks after he was gone she'd start to wonder how she ever imagined herself in love with him. Two weeks from the day he left, Lindy had made a giant card to tell him exactly the opposite had happened. If anything she loved him more than ever.

Over and over she had read the thick letter she'd received from him, until she had set each precious line in her memory. Rush's letters had been her lifeline to sanity.

The realization that he had received only a short one from her early after he sailed out of Bremerton, if that, was almost more than she could bear thinking about.

"What are you doing?" Steve asked, when Lindy reached for the phone.

"Calling Susan."

"What good is that going to do?"

"I...I don't know." But Lindy had to talk to someone before she went loony. Susan would know what to do.

"Hello?" Susan answered on the third ring, and Lindy could hear the twins crying in the background.

"Susan, it's Lindy. Something terrible has happened, and I don't know what to do." She was speaking as fast as she could, her voice raised and shaky.

"Lindy? Slow down. I can't understand a word you're saying."

"My letter to Rush came back," Lindy explained, doing her best to keep her voice as even as possible, although it wobbled like a toy top winding down after a long spin.

"Did you have the right address?"

Lindy reached for the envelope and read off Joanna's street numbers.

"Lindy," Susan muttered, interrupting her. "That's not the mailing address for the *Mitchell*."

"I know.... It's Joanna's. She said we were supposed to get all the mail to her by the fifteenth. Remember?"

"You weren't supposed to mail it to *her*," Susan cried. "It was supposed to be mailed, period."

"But I thought she was in charge of that."

"No, Lindy, Joanna doesn't have anything to do with the mail."

"Oh God, Susan, what will Rush think?"

Susan hesitated, then sighed. "It isn't that bad. I wouldn't worry about it, since it's only the one letter. He'll receive the others."

Lindy felt like weeping all the more. "But there was only the one letter. A long, long one.... Oh Susan, Rush must believe…I hate to even think about it. He'll assume I don't love him.''

The line was silent. "The important thing is not to panic.''

"I think it's too late for that.''

"Now calm down,'' Susan muttered, and Lindy could picture her friend chewing on her lower lip, trying to come up with something. "Jeff will tell him.''

"Tell him what?''

"Everything. How you've gotten involved in the wives' association and that we're seeing each other regularly. Rush is a smart man, Lindy. Give him credit for some intelligence.''

"Right,'' Lindy said, nodding her head once. "He'll figure it out…. He knows I love him.'' Lindy gnawed on her lip, remembering how the women's group had told her if she had any problems, she should contact Joanna.

A long silence stretched over the wire before Susan spoke. "Should I call Joanna or do you want to?''

The phone rang just after midnight. Lindy rolled onto her stomach and checked the time. She hadn't been sleeping well and had only turned off the light fifteen minutes before. The call was probably some prankster and she wasn't eager to answer it, figuring

Steve would. By the third ring, Lindy gave up on her brother and reached for the telephone receiver.

"Hello." She tried to make her voice sound as gruff and unfriendly as possible.

"This is a ham-radio operator in Anchorage, Alaska," the male voice explained. "A call is about to be transmitted to you from aboard the USS *Mitchell*. Talk as you would normally, but each time you're finished speaking you must say *over*. Do you understand?"

"Yes...."

"Okay. Go ahead and hang up and I'll connect you in about fifteen minutes."

Lindy's hand was shaking so badly she could barely replace the receiver. Rush. Somehow, some-way, Rush had found a means of contacting her. She scooted off the bed and paced barefoot across the carpet, waiting. Fifteen minutes had never seemed to drag by more slowly.

When the phone rang, she nearly tore it off the nightstand.

"Lindy? Over."

The line sounded as if it were coming from the moon. Static filled the air. Popping and hissing.

"Yes, this is Lindy. Over."

"I only want to know one thing. Are you pregnant? Over."

Chapter 12

"You want to know what? Over," Lindy asked incredulously.

"Are you pregnant or not? Over." Rush demanded a second time. The long distance wire popped and hissed, making it almost impossible to hear him clearly.

"Not. Stop yelling at me and let me explain."

Silence followed.

A third voice interrupted. "Over?"

"Over," Lindy repeated.

"I'm listening. Over." Some of the bitter anger was gone from Rush's voice, but his frustration and anxiety were evident even through the poor quality of the connection.

"There was a screwup with the letters. I'll explain it later. Over."

"Explain it now. Over."

"I mailed the letter to Joanna instead of the address you gave me. Over."

"Joanna who? Over."

"Joanna Boston. She's an ombudsman for the *Mitchell*. I thought she was handling all the correspondence. I didn't realize it would go through the normal channels. Over."

"In an entire month you only wrote me one letter? Over." The words were shouted into her ear.

"It was sixty-two pages long. Over." Lindy returned at equal volume.

Silence crackled like a morning breakfast cereal, and when Rush spoke again, his voice was more subdued, but still tense. "Do you regret the fact that we're married. Over."

"No. Do you? Over."

Rush seemed to take his own sweet time answering, and when he did his voice was almost a whisper. "Not now. Over."

"I love you," Lindy whispered, "I...I told you before you left that I know my own heart, and I do. Over."

"When I didn't get any mail, I thought you'd decided to...hell, I don't know what I thought. Over."

"I'll write every day, I promise. I'm not going to

make the same mistake twice with the mail business. Over.''

"Damn good thing. I nearly went berserk. Over.''

"I'm really sorry, Rush. I felt terrible when the letter was returned. Over.''

"I understand. Over.''

They were married and hadn't seen each other in two months and there didn't seem to be anything more they had to say.

"I have to go. Over," Rush said, after an awkward moment.

"I know. Goodbye, Rush. Don't worry about anything at this end. I'm doing okay. Your letters help.... I'm really sorry about what happened with yours. It won't happen again. Over.''

"Goodbye, Lindy. I need you. Over.''

The line went dead then and she was left holding the receiver in her hand. A tingling, burning feeling worked its way from her fingers down her arm and through her torso to settle in her stomach. Rush had been so angry with her. She couldn't blame him for being upset, but once that matter had been cleared up their conversation had remained awkward and stilted. They didn't have a lot to say to each other. His life was so far removed from hers now that there was nothing to share. He was a naval officer; she worked for an airline manufacturer. Their lives had briefly crossed paths for a three-week span and, when it came time to separate, they'd resisted and held on to each other. For the first time since Rush had been deployed, Lindy wondered if she had done the right thing in marrying him. At that moment it didn't feel right. Not for her, and from the way it sounded, not for Rush, either.

Lindy leaned back against the headboard and released a slow, agonized sigh. The shaking started then, and she gripped her hands together in a futile effort to control the trembling. She had married a man she barely knew, on an impulse. Doubts whizzed through her mind like buzzards circling a crippled animal, waiting for it to die. The picture was all too graphic in Lindy's troubled mind. She was stumbling and her family, particularly her brother, were all waiting for her to fall so they could tell her what a fool she'd been.

Lindy shook her head to dissolve the nightmarish image. She was being ridiculous. She loved Rush, and he loved her. He'd just ended their conversation by telling her of his need for her. A man like Rush Callaghan didn't say those words lightly. The circumstances they were trapped in had led to this negative thinking. These doubts would be gone by morning and she'd feel as strongly as ever about her commitment to Rush.

Swallowing at the hard lump in the back of her throat, Lindy turned off the bedside lamp and lay back down, resting her head on the pillow that had once been her husband's. Everything was going to work out fine. She'd done the right thing by marrying Rush. They were deeply in love with each other and if there were a few rocky roads ahead, that was to be expected. They'd weather those just fine.

But Lindy didn't sleep that night.

The tall waiter handed Lindy the oblong menu with the gold tassel. "This is a pleasant surprise," she said, looking across the linen-covered table at her older brother. Her relationship with Steve had gone much better this past month. He rarely mentioned Rush, and she stayed away from the subject of Carol. It wasn't exactly solid ground they stood on, but stable enough for the two of them to coexist without too many personality problems. The gesture of dinner was a delightful one, and Lindy wasn't about to refuse. They both needed a break from the humdrum of daily life.

These last couple of days Steve had been almost like his old self—teasing, joking and laughing. If she hadn't known him better, Lindy might have been fooled. She toyed with the idea of talking to Steve about the doubts that had been haunting her since the ship-to-shore call from Rush. She was terribly frightened that she'd done the wrong thing in marrying him, and she was unsure what, if anything, she could do about it.

"I figure I owe you at least one evening out before I leave,'' Steve said as a means of explanation for the unexpected invitation.

''You didn't need to pick the most expensive restaurant in town.''

Steve glanced over the top of his menu and shrugged. ''What else have I got to do with my money?''

''You could start dating again.'' She offered the suggestion flippantly, not really meaning it. Like Rush, Lindy had recognized almost immediately that her brother was still in love with his ex-wife.

''I could,'' Steve answered thoughtfully. ''But I won't.''

''I know,'' Lindy said, understanding perfectly.

''What do you know?''

It was almost as if they were children again, Lindy mused—the way his eyes sparkled with mischief and his mouth quirked with a teasing half smile.

''Well?'' he pressed.

''I know you won't date again.''

Slowly Steve set the menu aside, his fingers lingering over the gold tassel. The humor drained out of his eyes. ''The lobster sounds good, doesn't it?''

Lindy didn't want to introduce a subject that would embarrass or intimidate her older brother. Any mention of Carol was taboo and they both knew it. Sadly she recognized that talking over her fears about her marriage wasn't going to work, either. She didn't know what she'd tell Steve anyway. She was scared to death she'd married the wrong man, terrified that everything her brother had accused her of was true.

Her biggest concern was that she'd accepted Rush's proposal on the rebound and her marriage was based on emotional insecurity. Two weeks wasn't sufficient time to know a man well enough to commit her life to him. Even the regrets Rush had prophesied were beginning to come true. There were days when she had to struggle to remember what her husband looked like. A thousand unknowns haunted her. His phone call had only served to remind her how arrogant he could be, and the letters from him that had followed were filled with his angry frustration at not hearing from her.

Although Steve seemed more open than he had been, Lindy didn't feel she could discuss her doubts. Her brother was struggling with his own problems.

"Then lobster it is," she said, forcing her voice to sound airy and bright.

Steve picked up his butter knife and slowly ran the blade down his long fingers. "I wanted to take you to dinner for another reason, too."

"I'm a rotten cook and another night of my special enchiladas with homemade salsa was more than your stomach could tolerate?"

"Close," Steve answered, and chuckled. But his

eyes quickly sobered and he lowered his gaze. "Actually I owe you an apology, sis."

"Oh?" This was a major surprise.

"I was wrong to come down on you and Rush the way I did." He lay the butter knife down and reached for the salad fork, absently stroking the tines. Every mannerism revealed his regret at the way he'd chastised her earlier. "If I'd gone out and handpicked a husband for you, I couldn't have found a better man than Rush Callaghan."

Lindy's gaze rested on the delicate floral design of the place setting.

"You saw what you wanted," Steve continued, "and went after it. It takes a special kind of woman to do that, Lindy, and although I'll admit I had my fears, you've managed to calm every one of them."

"He is wonderful."

"You both are."

Lindy's nod was decidedly noncommittal. She could feel the emotion gathering in the back of her eyes. How could Steve sound so certain about her and Rush when she was struggling to believe in her own marriage? He made her happiness sound like a foregone conclusion when she was dog-paddling in a mire of self-doubts, struggling to stay afloat. A week before he would have taken her in his arms and comforted her. Tonight he made her sound like Joan of Arc for being so brave and true. There was no justice left in the world. None.

"Attribute my foul mood to the fact that I was shocked by your news. That and a strong brotherly instinct to protect my baby sister. I think the two of you are going to do exceptionally well together."

With trembling hands Lindy smoothed the pink linen napkin in her lap, hardly able to breathe normally, let alone find words to answer her brother. His original disdain for her and Rush's marriage had a lot more to do with his own unpleasant experience with nuptial bliss than anything else. Lindy's greatest fear was that she'd made the same mistake her brother had.

After an awkward moment, Lindy murmured, "I appreciate the apology, Steve, but it wasn't necessary."

Her brother shook his head, dismissing her words. "Rush will be good to you, and you're exactly the right kind of woman for him. I expect you'll both be very happy."

"We're going to try." The words were squeezed out of Lindy's throat. If he didn't stop soon, she was going to embarrass them both by bursting into tears.

"Give this marriage everything you've got, Lindy." He set down the fork and reached for the water glass. "Hold on to the happiness with both hands. Don't ever let anything stand between you."

His eyes were so full of pain that Lindy had to look away. She felt certain he must have read all the fear in her eyes. How sad it was that the two of them, who had once been so close, could sit across from each other and ignore what was on their hearts.

Reaching for the menu once more, Steve released his breath in a long sigh. "What do you say we start off dinner with a Caesar salad?"

"Sure," Lindy answered, forcing herself to smile.

My dearest Lindy,

I feel like a first-class idiot, shouting at you the way I did on the phone the other night. I jumped to conclusions, thinking the worst when I didn't get any mail from you. Lindy, I can't even begin to explain what was going on inside me. Jeff tried to tell me there was some logical explanation why you hadn't written, but I wouldn't listen. It was as though my greatest fears were hitting me in the face. I couldn't sleep; I couldn't eat. In my mind, I was absolutely certain Paul had come back and told you he'd made a mistake and you'd left with him. I know it sounds crazy now, but at the time, it made perfect sense.

From the day when the mail was handed out and I didn't get any, I've been acting like a real ass. Jeff must have gone to the chaplain because the next thing I knew I got called in to talk to him. He was the one who arranged the ship-to-shore call. Thank God he did.

After we talked, I was ready to free-fly. There's no way to explain how much better I felt. Has anyone ever told you what a sweet, sexy voice you have? And when you told me you still loved me, I nearly broke down and wept. I was so relieved. God, Lindy, I don't even know how to explain how good it felt to know everything's all right.

After the things I said to you in my last letter, I wouldn't blame you if you wanted to bag this whole marriage, but I'm hoping to God you don't. All I can say is, I'm sorry.

Honey, it's been less than three months and I'm already keeping track of how many days until I see you again. Try to arrange some additional time off in December, if you can, will you? I'm going to take you to bed and I swear it'll be a full week before we venture out of the bedroom. I guess that tells you how I'm feeling right now.

Before I met you I was this sane, ordinary man who was content with his life and sure of his goals. Two weeks after I meet you, and I'm a completely different person. There's a wedding band on my finger and I'm thinking about how nice it would be to become a father. I've even been toying with the idea of buying a house. What do you think? You can bet I do a lot of thinking about making love to my wife. Mostly I'm wondering what the hell I'm doing on the other side of the world.

I saw something yesterday that drove that point straight through my gut. We got orders to lend assistance to a Saudi oil tanker that had been hit by a Harpoon-type missile. One of our frigates pulled up alongside to help control the fire, and we sent a couple of Sea Kings with fire-fighting equipment and took their injured aboard. It really hit home that there could be trouble here, and this part of the world isn't sitting around enjoying crumpets and tea. I'm not telling you this to worry you, Lindy. I needed to see that burning tanker to take care of some business matters I should have done a long time before now. If anything happens to me, I want you to know you'll be well taken care of financially.

I've got to close this letter for now, but I'll write more later. Lots more. I love you, Lindy. It frightens me how much.

Dearest Rush,

Reading your latest letter was the best thing that's happened to me since our wedding. I've been feeling so confused and blue lately. After your letter, I felt like singing and dancing. I love you, husband. I don't have a single lingering doubt.

Did you hear the shouts of glee all across America this morning? No, we haven't landed on the moon or captured a Caribbean island. School started and those cries were the happy voices of mothers all over the land. At least, that's what Sandy and Mary and several of the other navy wives told me today. I've gotten to be good friends with several of them. Did you know that Sissy Crawford's real name isn't Sissy? It's something completely different, like An-

gela or Georgia. The other wives started calling her
that because she hates it so much when Bill's at sea,
and she's so sure everything's going to go wrong
that the women started calling her Sissy in a
friendly, teasing way. The name stuck. I don't know
if I should tell you what they've been calling me.
Actually it's kind of embarrassing, but by the same
token it's true. Randy. Don't worry. Susan made
them stop. Good grief, we could all call each other
that.

As for taking time off in December, you've got
it, fellow!

It's been over three months since you
sailed...were deployed. Are you impressed with the
navy lingo I'm picking up? Three months since we
kissed; three months since we made love; three
months since I've slept in your arms.

And another three to go.

I've got good news. I got a raise, which was a
pleasant surprise. I'm working out well with Boeing
and they seem to appreciate my obvious talents. I
decided to put the extra money in a savings account
so we'll have a little something to fall back on when
it's time for me to give up working to stay home
with the children. It's difficult for me to imagine
myself a mother when being a wife is still so new.
I don't think we need to rush into this parenting
business—do you? I wish we'd talked about these
matters before you left. I have no idea how you feel

about starting a family. When you asked if I was pregnant, it didn't exactly sound as if you'd have been pleased with the prospect if I had been.

Anyway, we're halfway through the tour and we've both managed to survive thus far. Susan and I and a bunch of other navy wives are celebrating Halfway Night this weekend. I don't know if I'm supposed to tell you this, so keep it under your hat because the other husbands are going to get insanely jealous. You, on the other hand, are sure to be cool-headed, mature and reasonable about this sort of thing, and I'm confident it isn't going to bother you.

The nine of us are carpooling it to a Seattle night-club to see some male strippers. Doesn't that sound like fun? Susan and I have been looking forward to this night for weeks. In fact we've had the reservations since the first week in August. As you've probably guessed, this is a popular club.

Believe me, Rush, you're not going to say anything that will frighten me anymore than I already am about what's happening in the Middle East. Reports are on the news every night. All I ask is that you take care of yourself.

Steve left Monday for a week of sea trials, so it's really been lonely around here. It's the first time I've been in the apartment completely alone since I arrived in Seattle. It gives me lots of time to write to you so I don't mind.

I suppose you know by now that Susan is pregnant. She's feeling surprisingly good, especially after the doctor confirmed that there's only one baby. Susan's hoping for a girl this time.

I'm going to mail this off since I don't want a repeat of what happened last month. Remember, I love you. Please don't take any crazy risks.

Lindy,
What the hell do you mean, you're going to see a male strip show! You're damn right I didn't tell the others. Good God, they'd stage a mutiny. As for me being mature and coolheaded, you couldn't be more wrong. I don't like it. Not one damn bit.

My dearest, darling Rush,
The male strippers were sexy as hell. What gorgeous bodies! What cute buns. What attractive…never mind. We had a fantastic time, but, quite honestly, it was too much for us men-starved navy wives. We talked it over and agreed this kind of entertainment would be better served later in the tour when we could count on our husbands being home soon. We decided to go back for a Final Fling the week before the *Mitchell* is scheduled to arrive home.

I love you, Rush Callaghan. Take care of yourself.

Love,
Lindy

P.S. Would you ever consider wearing spurs and a cute little cowboy hat to bed?

"Line 314," Lindy murmured absently, answering the phone at her desk.

"Lindy, it's Steve."

Something in the pitch of her brother's low-modulated voice, something in the way he said her name instantly alerted Lindy. Goose bumps shot up and down her spine. Not once in all the weeks that Lindy had worked for Boeing had her brother telephoned the office. She didn't even know where he'd gotten her work number.

"What's wrong?"

Steve hesitated. "I just heard a news bulletin over the radio. There's been a report of an accident aboard the *Mitchell*."

"Oh, God." The words were wrenched from her heart. "Rush.... Did they say anything about Rush?"

"No, but it's much too soon. Don't panic, Lindy. There are nearly four thousand men aboard the carrier. The chance of Rush being a fatality is minute."

Lindy closed her eyes and cupped her hand over her mouth as terror gripped her. Her heart roared in her chest so loudly that it nearly drowned out her brother's words.

"I think it would be a good idea if you left work and met me at the apartment."

She nodded, unable to find her voice.

"Lindy?"

"I'm on my way." Already she was clearing her

computer terminal, doing only what was absolutely necessary so she could leave.

"Lindy, can you drive? Do you want me to come get you?"

"No.... I'm fine. When did it happen? How?"

"They're not exactly sure, but the preliminary reports are mentioning a plane crash."

"How many are dead?"

"Sweetie, listen. The only reason I phoned was so you wouldn't hear the news yourself or from someone at the office and panic. I'm telling you everything I know. I called the base and they're setting up an information center for wives and family. Once you're home I'll take you there."

"I'll meet you as soon as I can." Worry had already clogged Lindy's throat by the time she replaced the receiver. Her supervisor was just walking into her office when Lindy scooted her chair back from the desk.

"You heard? Someone just told me there was something about the *Mitchell* on the radio. Take whatever time you need."

"Thanks." Lindy grabbed her purse, her legs so weak she could hardly walk.

The drive from Renton to the apartment normally took fifteen to twenty minutes. Lindy made it in ten and had little memory of the ride. She dared not turn on the radio for fear of what she'd learn. The entire time she was driving, she prayed, mumbling the same desperate plea over and over again. An aircraft carrier was a huge ship, a city unto itself, able to house as many as six thousand men. The possibility of Rush being a fatality was infinitesimal. He was the chief navigator. The bridge was possibly the safest place of all. He would be free from harm. At least that was what Lindy kept telling herself.

Steve was waiting for her when she burst in the front door. "Did you learn anything more?"

He looked terribly pale, and nodded. "Lindy, sit down."

"*No!*" she screamed, knotting her fists. "Tell me! Is he dead? Is he?"

Steve raked his hands through his hair. "I don't know. Apparently an Intruder was landing and a wing caught on the arresting gear. It cartwheeled on the flight deck, spewing wreckage," he hesitated. "They haven't released any names yet. Five are known dead."

"Dear God."

Her brother placed his hands on her shoulders and his eyes revealed his own personal torment. She knew in that minute that he would have given his soul not to be the one to tell her this.

"What is it?" she asked, in a voice that was as calm and as accepting as she could make it.

"The latest information reports that part of the plane careened into the bridge."

Lindy shut her eyes and it was the last thing she

should have done. Instantly she felt her legs give out as her mind conjured up the worst possible scene of bodies being hurled through space and men screaming in agony. Fire seemed to have erupted everywhere. Lindy gasped and her hands shot out.

Steve managed to catch her, pressing her head against his shoulder. "Rush is going to be all right," he murmured, while his hand smoothed her hair.

"No," she said, in a whisperlike sound. "He isn't." If there was any action or any trouble, Rush would be there right in the middle of it.

Steve escorted Lindy to the naval base, where an information center had been set up. The first person Lindy saw was Susan. The two women looked at each other and started sobbing. Timmy and Tommy, not knowing what to make of everything, were soon crying, too. Lindy took Tommy and attempted to comfort him, but the youngster wanted his mother and squirmed in Lindy's arms.

"Jeff?" Lindy finally managed to ask.

"I don't know. What about Rush?"

Lindy heaved in a calming breath. "I haven't heard."

It seemed hours passed before any additional information was released, and then the names of the injured were read. Neither Jeff nor Rush were listed. Lindy didn't know whether to be happy or terrified. The only choices that remained were that both men had somehow magically escaped the explosion or were among those listed as dead.

Steve was at Lindy's side as much as possible, doing what he could. One look at her brother told Lindy he suspected the worst. As much as she could, Lindy tried to be positive. If Rush had died in the explosion, she reasoned, she would have felt it. Deep within her heart, she would have felt a part of herself die. She wouldn't be this calm, this accepting.

People milled around everywhere. Wives, children, parents. Rather than sit and worry, Lindy mingled with the others, talking, praying and crying— sometimes all three at once.

It was when she turned to find Steve at her side that she knew word had finally come through. She looked up to the brother she had always loved, the brother who had shielded her from whatever pain he could, and Lindy smiled. She realized at the time how odd that was.

Her brother slipped his arm around her shoulder and his jaw jutted out in a gesture of grief and pain.

"Rush is listed as missing."

Chapter 13

"What do you mean missing?" Lindy asked. "Rush couldn't have just disappeared." It astonished her how calm she felt, how controlled, as though they were discussing something as mundane as the tide tables or what to fix for dinner.

"Lindy, I think you should prepare yourself for the worst."

"That would be silly," she said, turning back to the little boy she'd been talking to and purposely ignoring her brother. "Rush is fine. I know he is. There's been some screwup and he's going to be furious when he learns the way the navy has everyone so worried about him."

"Lindy...." Steve hesitated, and his brow creased

in thick folds of concern and regret. "I hope to God you're right."

"Of course I am."

Steve left her then and Lindy sank into an empty chair. Her hands shook so badly that she clenched them together in her lap, her long nails cutting crescents of pain into her palms. Soon her arms were shaking, then her legs, until her whole body felt as if it were consumed by uncontrollable spasms.

Susan took the chair beside Lindy and wrapped her own sweater around Lindy's shoulders. Susan held it there until some of the intense cold she was experiencing seeped away and a steady warmth invaded her limbs.

Lindy tried to smile, failed, and whispered one word. "Jeff?"

"He's fine."

Lindy nodded once. "Good."

"They'll find him, Lindy," Susan said, her voice thick with conviction, although she was struggling with her own fears. "I know they will. Jeff won't let anyone rest until they do."

"I know." Lindy remembered how Susan had once told her that she didn't worry so much about Jeff at sea because she always knew Rush would be there to watch out for her husband. The truth of what Susan was telling her now was the only slender thread Lindy had to hang on to. Jeff would turn hell

upside down until he learned what had happened to
Rush.

Soon the other wives joined Lindy, scooting their
chairs and forming a protective circle around her.
No one did much talking. No one tried to build her
up with false hopes. No one suggested she try to eat
or get some sleep. Or leave.

That night cots were brought into the information
center for those who wished to stay. Lindy insisted
the other wives go back to their families, but each
one in turn refused. They were special sisters,
bonded together in ways that were thicker than
blood.

"No one's leaving until we find out what happened to Rush," Susan said, speaking for them all.

The others managed to sleep that night in the cots
provided. Lindy tried, but couldn't. Every time she
closed her eyes that same terrible scene flashed
through her mind, and she was convinced she could
hear Rush cry out in torment. As the hours slowly,
methodically ticked away, Lindy sat and stared into
space. In the darkest part of the night, surrounded
by silence, she tried to prepare herself to accept
Rush's death, but every time she entertained the notion, such piercing pain stabbed through her that she
shoved the thought from her mind. This interminа-
ble waiting was the worst nightmare of her life.

Food was brought in the following morning and

the others ate, but Lindy knew it would be impossible for her to hold anything down.

Susan handed her a glass of orange juice. "You didn't eat anything yesterday. Try this," she said softly, insistently. "You're going to need your strength."

Lindy wanted to argue with her friend but hadn't the fortitude. "Okay."

Another eternity passed, a lifetime—hours that felt like years, minutes that dragged like weeks, seconds that could have been days. And still they waited.

"He's dead," Lindy sobbed to the others late that afternoon, although just saying the words aloud nearly crippled her. "I know it. I can feel it in my heart. He's gone."

"You don't know it," Susan argued, and her own eyes shone brightly with unshed tears. Her hands trembled and she laced her fingers together as though offering a silent prayer.

"Don't even say it," Sissy cried, her face streaked with moisture.

Joanna gripped Lindy's fingers with her own and knelt in front of her, her gaze holding Lindy's. "He's alive until we know otherwise. Hold tight to that, Lindy. It's all we've got."

Lindy nodded, her eyes so blurred with tears that when she looked up to find her brother standing over

her, she couldn't read his expression. A powerful
magnetic force drove her to her feet.

"Tell me," she whispered urgently. "Tell me."

"He's alive."

Lindy didn't hear anything more than that before
she broke down and started to weep, covering her
face with her hands, her shoulders heaving with the
depth of her relief. But these tears were ones of joy.
A sheer release from the endless unknown. She
tossed her arms around her brother's neck and he
gripped her waist and swung her around. Susan and
the others were jumping up and down, hugging each
other, laughing and crying as well.

When everyone had settled back down, Steve
gave them the rest of the information. "They found
Rush buried under a pile of rubble; he's lost a lot
of blood and in addition to internal injuries, his arm
has been severely cut. He's being flown to Tripler
Army Hospital in Hawaii for microsurgery. Apparently the nerves in his left arm were severed. He's
unconscious, but alive."

"I'm going to him," Lindy said with raw determination, as though she expected an argument.
Nothing would stop her. She wouldn't believe Rush
was going to live until she saw him herself. Touched
him. Kissed him. Loved him.

Steve nodded. "I already made arrangements for
you to fly out today."

* * *

A pumpkin and a picture of a witch decorating the wall across the room from him were the first things Rush noticed when he opened his eyes. His mouth was as dry as Arizona in August and his head throbbed unmercifully. A hospital, he determined, but he hadn't any idea where.

Carefully and with a great deal of effort, he rolled his head to one side and stared at the raised rail of the bed. He blinked, sure he was imagining the vision that was before him.

"Lindy?"

The apparition didn't move. Her fingers were gripping the steel railing and her forehead was pressed against the back of her hands. She looked as though she were sleeping.

Rush tried to reach out and touch her, gently wake her, but he couldn't lift his arm. Even the effort sent a sharp shooting pain through his shoulder. He must have groaned because Lindy jerked her head up, her eyes wide with concern. When she saw he was awake, she sighed and grinned. Rush swore he'd never seen a more beautiful smile in his life. The pain that stabbed through him with every breath was gone. The ache in his head vanished as the look in his wife's eyes immersed him in an unspeakable joy that transcended everything else.

"You're real," he murmured. He refused to believe that she was a figment of his imagination. His head remained fuzzy and his vision blurred, but Lindy was real. He'd stake his life on that.

She nodded and her hand brushed lightly over his face, lovingly caressing his jaw. "And you're alive. Oh, Rush, I nearly lost you."

She bit into her bottom lip and Rush knew she was struggling not to cry. He wished he could have spared her all worry and doubt.

"Where am I...? How long?"

"You're in a hospital in Hawaii. Two days now."

He frowned. "That long?" Now that his eyesight was clearing, he could see the dark smudges under Lindy's eyes. She was as pale as death, as though recovering from a bad bout of flu. And much thinner than he remembered. Too thin. "You look terrible."

She laughed, and the sweet, lilting sound wrapped itself around his heart, squeezing emotion from him. Dear God, he loved Lindy. So much of the accident remained clouded in his mind. All he could remember was hearing a horrendous noise and seeing a ball of fire come hurling toward him. Everything had happened so fast that there had barely been time to do anything more than react. All he knew was that he didn't want to die. He wanted to go home to Lindy. His Lindy. His love.

The next thing he remembered was pain. Terrible pain. More acute than anything he'd ever experienced. He knew he was close to dying, knew he might not make it, and still all he could think about was Lindy. Dying would have stopped the agony; slipping into the dark swirling void of death would have been welcome if only it would end the torment, but Rush chose the pain because he knew it would lead him back to Lindy.

"Have you looked in a mirror lately?" she asked, her lips twitching with a teasing smile. "You're not exactly ready to be cast as Prince Charming yourself."

"You've been sick?" he pressed, his tongue faltering over the words. It was a struggle to keep awake, the pull back to unconsciousness greater with each second.

"No, just worried. It took them nearly forty hours to find you after the accident and until then you were listed as missing."

"Oh God, Lindy, I'm...sorry."

"I'm fine now that I know you're going to be all right." Again her fingers touched his face, smoothing the hair from his brow, lingering as though she needed the reassurance that he was real.

"How many...dead?"

"Seven. Three on the flight deck and four on the bridge."

Rush's jaw tightened. "Who?"

Lindy recited the names and each one fell upon his chest like a boulder dropped from the ceiling. "...good men," he said after a moment, and was shocked at how fragile his voice sounded.

"More than twenty suffered serious injuries."

Rush felt himself drifting off; he resisted, but the pull of the tide was too powerful for him to fight. "How bad..."

"The burn victims are the worst."

He nodded and that was the last he remembered.

When he woke again the room was pitch-dark. He felt a straw at his mouth and he sucked greedily. "What time is it?"

"Two a.m."

"Lindy, is that you?"

"Do you need something for the pain?"

He shook his head. "No." Her fingers curled around his own and he held on to her, savoring her touch. He slept again.

Lindy sat in a chair at her husband's side. She'd tried to sleep countless times, but the rest her body craved continued to elude her. Just as she'd start to drift off, the horror of those two days of not knowing if Rush was dead or alive returned and snapped her awake. She'd come so close to losing him. Seven men had died. Honorable men. And Rush had come a hairsbreadth from making the count eight. The men who had died were husbands, fathers, lovers—and now they were gone.

Standing, she walked over to the window. Palm trees swayed in the late afternoon breeze. The sun shone and the ocean lapped relentlessly against the white, sandy beach. The flawless beauty of the scene should have soothed her troubled spirit, but it didn't. Instead she felt a cold hard feeling settle in her lungs. It spread out, making her breathing labored and causing her throat to ache. Those men had died, and for what? Lindy had no answers, and every time she closed her eyes the questions started to pound at her, demanding answers when she had none.

"Lindy?"

She took a minute to compose herself, pasted a smile on her face and turned around. "So Sleeping Ugly is finally awake. How are you feeling?"

"You don't want to know."

Concern moved her to his bedside. "Should I get the nurse? She said if you needed something for pain, I could..."

"I'm doing okay." His brows folded into a tight frown as he looked up at her. "You're still looking like death warmed over."

She forced a cheery laugh and decided to put her makeup on with a heavier hand before her next visit. "That's a fine thing to say to me!"

"When was the last time you had a decent meal?"

She opened her mouth to tell him, but paused when she realized she didn't know herself. "I'm fine, Rush. You're the patient here, not me."

He looked for a minute as if he were going to

argue with her, but he didn't. "If you're not hungry, I am."

"I'll see what I can scrounge up."

She returned a few minutes later, carrying a tray. But it was soon apparent that Rush had no appetite and had used the excuse of hunger as a ploy to get her to sample something.

Three days passed. Rush grew stronger with each one, and Lindy grew paler and thinner. She still couldn't sleep—not more than an hour at a stretch.

A week after Rush arrived in Hawaii, Lindy strolled into his hospital room to discover her husband sitting up for the first time. His left arm was in a cast and hung in a sling over his chest. The swelling in his face had gone down considerably, and he looked almost like his old handsome self once more. Lindy paused and smiled, perhaps her first genuine one since she'd arrived in this tropical paradise.

"You're looking fit."

"Come here, wife," he said holding out his one good arm to her. "I'm tired of those skimpy pecks on the cheek you've been giving me. I'm starved for you."

Lindy walked across the room like a woman who'd been wandering in the desert and been offered a glass of water. Once Rush had his arm around her, his mouth claiming hers, she felt whole again. He smelled incredibly good and tasted of peppermint.

The fears and doubts that had been hounding her all week dissolved in the warmth of his hold. When he lifted his head and smiled, Lindy felt weak and breathless in his embrace.

"Lindy, dear God, I've nearly died, I've wanted to hold you so much."

Angry, selfish thoughts flooded her mind, and she clamped her mouth shut. He'd nearly died, yes, but it was from a terrible plane crash and explosion that didn't have anything to do with her. But when Rush directed her mouth to his, she was engulfed in his kiss, lost and drowning. Nothing else mattered. As his lips closed over hers, demanding and hungry, he reclaimed everything that had once been his: her heart, her body, her soul. There was nothing left inside her to protest. He owned her so completely, so unquestionably, that she hadn't the will to say or do anything. All she could do was submit.

She wrapped her arms around his neck and leaned into him, giving him her tongue when he sought it, taking his when it was offered. Their need for each other was urgent. Fierce. Savage, yet tender. Nothing else in the world made sense except this. Only the driving need Lindy felt to be a part of Rush.

Moisture appeared in the corners of her eyes and Rush sipped away her tears. He kissed her eyes, her forehead, her cheeks, her lips, and nuzzled tenderly at her neck while his fingers tunneled through her dark hair.

"Lindy," he breathed. "My love, my own sweet love." His long fingers brushed the wisps of bangs from her face and wiped away the last trace of tears, as though she was the most precious thing he had ever touched.

"I talked to the doctor this morning," he whispered. "I'm going to be released at the end of the week."

Lindy's tender heart swelled with unrestrained joy.

"We have one night, love, just one night before I fly back to the *Mitchell*."

For one frenzied moment, Lindy was sure she'd heard him incorrectly. Going back? He couldn't possibly be returning to the Persian Gulf after what had happened.

"No." She freed herself from his grip and took a step back. "You can't go back!"

"Honey, I have to. It's my job."

"But…"

"What did you expect me to do?"

Lindy wasn't sure what she'd assumed would happen. Anything but having him return to the same nightmare.

"Honey, listen. We've only got six weeks of the cruise left. Hell, for all I know we could even be headed back sooner than that, depending on the amount of damage we sustained. Six weeks isn't such a long time. I'll be home before you know it.''

Somehow Lindy managed to nod. They had precious time left, and the thought of spending these last days together arguing was intolerable. After all, there wasn't much she could say. She'd thought— or at least hoped—he'd be coming home with her now. She needed him sleeping at her side to chase away the demons and dissolve the horror from her mind.

Rush may want to make love to her, Lindy realized, but he wanted to get back to his ship more. She'd noted that when he started talking about the *Mitchell* his eyes had seemed to spark with new life. He didn't like lying around the hospital; she would have been surprised if he had. Rush longed to go back to his ship, back to his men. He wanted to leave her behind, safely tucked away in a Seattle apartment while he was gallivanting all over the world, risking his life. Risking her peace of mind. Risking their happiness.

"I hope that hotel room of yours has a double bed," Rush said, smiling up at her.

"It does," she assured him, averting her gaze to the scene outside the window.

Something was wrong with Lindy. Rush knew it, felt it every time she walked in the room. She looked a little better—at least he knew she was eating reg-

ularly. Some color had returned to her pale cheeks
when they'd walked in the sunshine.

Rush tried to draw her out, tried to get her to tell
him what was troubling her, but she held it all inside
and he didn't press her. He would be leaving the
hospital early that afternoon and leaving Lindy first
thing in the morning. She'd been through a great
deal and so had he. If what was bothering her was
important, she'd say something to him.

The petite blond nurse who had been assigned his
room strolled in, holding a small white cup and a
glass of water. She was young and pretty, the kind
of woman who might have attracted his attention
before he met Lindy. Now he only had eyes for his
wife and barely gave the woman more than a second
glance.

"Pill time," she announced cheerfully.

Rush grumbled and held out his hand. The blue-
eyed nurse waited while he took the two capsules
and swallowed down a glass of water.

"Where's your wife this afternoon?"

"She'll be by later," Rush explained. He was surprised Lindy wasn't there all ready. Lindy was as
keen as he was to get out of this sterile environment,
but he was far more eager to get his wife into bed.
One damn night was all they had. He wished to hell
it could be more. It seemed their entire married life
had been crammed into three all-too-short nights.

"I hear you're leaving us."

He nodded. He didn't like the antiseptic smell here, and he swore the food must taste better in prison. It had been torture to be this close to the ocean, to smell the clean tangy scent of it and be prohibited from doing anything more than gaze at the blue waters. He was anxious to get back to the *Mitchell*. He felt a lot like someone who had fallen off a horse and needed to climb right back on again. He'd been mentally shaken by the accident, his courage tested. He needed to set foot on the bridge, look down on that flight deck and know he was in control once more.

"I don't know when I've seen a woman more in love with her husband. Or more worried," the pretty blond nurse went on to say. "When your wife first arrived, I thought we were going to have to admit her. I swear she was as pale as bleached flour. I suppose you know she wouldn't leave your side. For three days, she didn't move. The doctors tried repeatedly to assure her you were going to be all right, but she wouldn't believe it. Not until you woke, and even then she refused to go."

Rush rested his head against the thin pillow and held in a sigh until his chest ached with the effort. He'd known that every time he woke Lindy had been with him, but he hadn't realized she'd spent every minute at his side.

"I hope you appreciate that woman," the nurse continued.

"I do," Rush countered. Tonight he'd show Lindy just how much.

Lindy was determined that this one night with Rush would be as perfect as she could make it. She planned to blot out all her doubts and grab hold of what happiness she could before Rush returned to the Persian Gulf. She yearned to encapsulate these last hours together and hold them in her memory until he returned safely to her in December.

"How are you feeling?" she asked, once they were inside her hotel room.

"A little weak," Rush admitted reluctantly. "But I'm getting stronger every day."

She helped him into a chair. It was on the tip of her tongue to suggest he wait a few more days before flying across the world and rejoining his ship, but she knew it would be useless. She knew Rush. She'd seen that hard look of determination he wore more than once. He wouldn't listen to her.

"I thought we'd order dinner from room service," she said, standing awkwardly in the middle of the floor.

He nodded. "Good idea." He hesitated and gave her a look that was almost shy. "I have another good idea, too. Come to me, Lindy. I need you."

She couldn't have refused him had her life depended on it. He stood, reached for her hand and walked her to the bed. He kissed her once, hard, his tongue delving into her mouth, stroking hers. His right hand was fumbling with the buttons of her blouse, but the left one was incapable of giving much assistance. With their mouths still linked, Lindy brushed his hand aside and helped him. When she was finished with her own, she freed his uniform shirt from his waistband and unbuttoned it for him.

"Thanks," Rush breathed hoarsely, when she'd finished the task. Lindy paused, biting her lip as she ran her hand over the dark-furred chest. The muscles of his abdomen felt hard and sleek, the curling hairs wispy against the tips of her fingers.

"I want you like hell," he groaned.

Lindy let her eyes fall and released a short, delicate chuckle. "I can tell." His free hand cupped her breast and her nipple blossomed and grew incredibly hard. "I want you, too."

He flicked his thumb over the rose tip of her breast and she moaned.

"I can tell," he repeated thickly.

They finished undressing each other with trembling hands. Lindy helped Rush with the parts he couldn't manage, and he helped her the best he could. Soon they were lying on the mattress, their bodies on fire for each other.

When he moved on top of her, Lindy smiled up at him, craving the fiery release his body would give her. Still trembling, she closed her eyes and gave herself over to this experience. She allowed herself

to be swallowed up in his tenderness, and when he
entered her, her body answered in perfect counter-
point to his. Rush's touch, his lovemaking, was a
balm, a healing potion for all they had suffered.
Tears wet her face and his lips found them. Intuitively he knew she needed assurances and he gave
them to her with the ebb and flow of his body into
her own. No matter what the future held, he seemed
to be telling her, no matter what happened in the
next six weeks, they would have this night to hold
on to and to remember.

They made love again after dinner, and he held
and kissed her long after midnight. While Rush
soundly slept, Lindy climbed out of bed and cuddled
up in the chair across from him.

She'd tried so hard to put the fear behind her, but
she couldn't. A hundred times in the past week,
she'd hungered to tell him how she'd nearly gone
crazy with worry, and she hadn't said a word. She
wanted to explain how every time she closed her
eyes the same freakish nightmare haunted her sleep.
But again and again she'd held her tongue, gliding
over what was important for fear of shattering the
peace of these past days together.

In a few hours Rush would return to his ship and
she would go back to Seattle. She'd been wrong not
to tell Rush what she was feeling, wrong to allow
him to assume she could go on playing this charade.
Steve was right. He had been all along—she

wouldn't make a good navy wife. It wasn't in her to bid her husband farewell time after time and handle whatever crisis befell them with calm acceptance.

Twice now Lindy had found herself deeply in love, convinced she knew her own heart each time. Confident enough to wear the rings each man had given her. Both times she'd been wrong. She wasn't the type of woman Rush needed. She wasn't strong enough to endure months of loneliness and deal with the knowledge that she would always take second place in her husband's life.

Hot tears scalded her eyes and when she could restrain them no longer, she let them flow freely down her face, no longer willing to hold them back.

Rush raised his head from the pillow, looking disoriented and groggy. He turned and stared at his sobbing wife.

"Lindy," he breathed her name into the night. "What's wrong?"

"Do you love me, Rush?"

"Of course I do." He threw back the sheet and sat on the edge of the bed. "You know I do."

"If you love me...if you really love me, you'll understand...." She paused.

Rush moved off the bed, knelt down in front of her and took her two hands in his one. "Understand what, honey?"

"I want you to get out of the navy."

He tossed his head back as if she'd slapped him. "Lindy, you don't know what you're asking."

"I do know. I know you love it. I know you've always loved being on the sea. But there are other jobs, other ways.... I can't bear this, Rush, not knowing from one day to the next if you're going to be dead or alive. Let some other man put his life on the line. Someone without a wife. Anyone but you."

"Lindy—oh love." He pressed his forehead on her bent knee and seemed to be pulling his thoughts together. When he raised his head, his eyes were hard. "The navy is my life. It's where I belong. I can't walk away from a fifteen-year commitment because you're afraid I'm going to be injured again."

Lindy felt as though her heart were crumbling, the emotional agony was so intense. She pulled her hands free of his grasp and stiffened. "Then you leave me no choice."

Chapter 14

"I don't leave you any choice? What do mean by that?" Rush demanded.

Lindy didn't know. All she did know was that everything the other wives had warned her about was happening. Rush and she had such little time together and, not wanting to say or do anything to disrupt these precious few days, Lindy had skimmed the surface of their relationship, ignoring the deep waters of unhappiness and strife. They'd avoided any chance of conflict in their marriage until everything was ready to burst inside her.

"Well?" he repeated.

"I don't know," she admitted reluctantly. "I want you to do something else with your life. Something outside of the navy that isn't dangerous. You've got me to think about now...and children later. Maybe you think I'm being selfish, but I want you to be a husband and father before anything else. The navy is first with you now and I'll always be a poor second. I hate it.''

Rush rammed his fingers through his hair. ''Honey, you can't change a man from what he already is. You don't have any idea what you're asking me to do—it'd be impossible.''

''You don't seem to understand what you want of *me*,'' she countered sharply. ''You claim you love me. You claim you want our marriage to work. But I'll always play second fiddle in your life, and I can't. I just can't deal with that. If playing hero is so important to you, then fine.''

Rush's lips tightened and he stood and walked away from her.

''I love you, Rush.'' Her voice was taut, strangled. ''All I'm asking is for you to love me as much as I do you.''

''I do love you,'' he shouted.

''No.'' She shook her head with such force that her hair went swirling around her face. ''You love the navy more.''

''It's been my life for fifteen years.''

''I want to be your life now.''

''God, Lindy, you want me to give up everything that's ever been important to me.'' He threw back his head as a man in agony would, closed his eyes and then glared at the dark ceiling.

Lindy bounced her index finger against her chest. "I want to be the most important person in your life."

"You are!"

"No," she murmured sadly. "I'm not. Look at you. You nearly died on that stupid aircraft carrier and you can hardly wait to get back. I can feel the restlessness in you. It's like you've got to prove something."

Rush whirled around to face her then, his eyes wide, his body taut. "You knew what I was when we got married. You were perfectly aware how I felt about the navy then. You were willing to accept it as my career. What happened to that unshakable confidence you had that we were doing the right thing to rush into marriage? Lord, I can't believe this."

"I was confident I loved you. I'm sure of it now."

"The navy is part of me, Lindy. A big part of who and what I am. Don't you see that?"

"No." Her voice cracked, and she sobbed once.

The sight of her tears seemed to tear at him and Rush knelt beside her and pulled her into one arm, holding her tightly, as though he felt her pain and was desperate to do anything he could to alleviate it. Lindy wept against his shoulder, her arms moving up and clinging to his neck. His mouth sought and found hers and he kissed her into submission while his hand worked its magic on her body, destroying her will to argue.

Before Lindy knew what was happening, Rush had her back in bed and his mouth was sucking on her breast; he was tormenting her nipples with his tongue, and she was being devoured by the licking flames of desire.

"No...no," she sobbed, and pushed him away. She jumped out of bed, her shoulders heaving with the effort it had cost her to leave his arms. "You aren't going to use me this way!"

Rush rolled on his back and closed his eyes in angry frustration. "Use you! Now it's a sin to make love to you, too?"

"It is when you use lovemaking to bury an issue."

"Can you blame me?" he shouted, his patience obviously on a short fuse. "I'm flying out of here shortly. I won't see you until the middle of December—if then, from the way you're talking. I'd prefer that we spend our last hours making love, not fighting. If that's such a terrible crime, then I'm guilty."

The alarm rang, and the tinny sound echoed around the room, startling them both. Lindy glared accusingly at the clock radio. Already it was time for Rush to leave her, and she hadn't said even half of what was in her heart.

Without a word her husband climbed out of bed

and started dressing in his uniform. He had some difficulty, with his left arm in a cast, but he didn't seek her help, and she didn't offer.

Numb with pain and disbelief, Lindy watched him. Nothing she'd said had mattered to him. Not one word had seemed to reach him. He was so intent on getting back to the *Mitchell* that nothing, not her love, not her demands or her pleas, was important enough to delay him.

Once he finished buttoning his shirt, Rush picked up his things that littered the room, preparing to leave.

Lindy hated the way he ignored her so completely. For all the notice he gave her, she might as well have been an empty beer can. Savored for the moment of pleasure it brought, discarded once used.

She was kneeling in the middle of their bed, and the tears streaked her face. "It's either the navy or me," she said, and her voice wobbled as she struggled not to beg him.

Rush paused at the door, his hand on the knob, but he didn't turn around to look at her. "I love you, Lindy, but I can't change what I am because of your fears. I could leave the navy, but it wouldn't be the right decision for either of us. If you're going to force me to decide, then I have to go with what I am."

Lindy felt as though he'd struck her. She closed her eyes and covered her face with both hands. The door of the hotel room opened, and desperate now, she scooted off the bed. "Rush."

He paused.

"When the *Mitchell* returns, I won't be on that dock waiting for you!" She shouted the words at him, in a voice that was threatening as a shark's jaw. "I mean it. I won't be there."

His shoulders were stiff, his head held high and proud. "Then I won't expect you," he said, and walked away from her without looking back.

Steve was waiting for Lindy when she stepped out of the jetway that led into the interior of Sea-Tac Airport. He brushed a quick kiss over her cheek and took the carry-on bag from her hand. When he lifted his head and looked at her, he paused and frowned.

"How was the flight?"

Lindy shrugged, praying she didn't look as bad as she felt. "Fine."

"How's Rush?"

"He couldn't be better," she answered, unable to keep her voice from dipping with heavy sarcasm. "He's all navy—you know him. God, country, apple pie—the whole patriotic bit. He nearly lost his arm. He nearly bled to death, but he couldn't enjoy a few days in paradise because it was more important for him to get back to the *Mitchell*. He's got a job to do, you know. He alone is going to uphold world peace. You didn't tell me what a hero I married, Steve.''

Looking stunned, her brother stopped and glared at her, his eyes wide and filled with surprise. ''Exactly what is your problem?''

''Nothing,'' she flared. ''Everything,'' she amended.

''What happened?''

She didn't want Steve to be gentle and concerned. Not when she was being forced to admit her blunder. ''You were right from the first. I made a mistake.... A bad one. I'm not the kind of woman who will ever make a good navy wife.... You knew that from the beginning.''

Steve's frown deepened. ''I've come to think differently in the past few weeks. Lindy, when we got the news there'd been an accident aboard the *Mitchell*, you were as solid as a rock. It was me who fell apart at the seams. Don't you remember how I kept telling you you should prepare yourself for the worst? Everything I said and did was wrong. You were like an anchor during that whole time. I was the one leaning on you for strength.''

Lindy's smile was weak and gentle as she placed her hand on her brother's forearm. ''You were wonderful. I thank God you were there.''

''But you love Rush. Dear God, Lindy, you were so strong and brave when we learned he was missing, and yet I was afraid it would have killed you if the damage control party hadn't found Rush in time."

"Yes, I love him. But I'm not willing to take second place in his life. With Rush—" she paused and looked up at him, her gaze narrowing "—and with *you*, the navy will always come first."

"Did you tell Rush this?"

She nodded, and her eyes filled with an unspeakable sadness. "He knows exactly how I feel."

"What are you going to do now?"

"I...I don't know."

Steve placed his free arm around her shoulder and squeezed gently. "Don't decide anything yet. You're hurting and miserable. You've got several weeks to think matters through and then, once Rush is safely back in Seattle, you two can sort things out."

"I told Rush I wouldn't be there to meet him when the *Mitchell* sails home. I meant it, Steve. He put the navy first. He was the one who chose his career over me."

Steve's mouth and eyes thinned with frustration. "You sent Rush back to the *Mitchell* with that piece of good news? Come on, Lindy. It's time to grow up here. So you were worried about him. That's only natural. But don't try to suffocate him now because eventually it'll kill your marriage. Rush isn't the kind of man who's going to let someone else dictate his life. You knew that when you agreed to be his wife.''

Lindy pulled herself free from her brother's hold. ''I didn't expect you to understand.''

''For God's sake, Lindy, you want to castrate a man because he's got a job to do and feels honor-bound to do it? What kind of logic is that?''

''I'm not going to talk about it anymore.'' Quick-paced, determined steps carried her down the concourse and away from her brother. She should have known better than to even try to talk to him. Steve Kyle was as much into patriot games as Rush.

''Lindy,'' her brother called, catching up with her. ''I can't let you ruin your life like this—and Rush's in the process. Any idiot can see how much you two love each other.''

''I don't want to hear this. It's none of your business, so keep your opinions to yourself.''

''I can't!''

''Get your own house in order, big brother, and then you can start cleaning mine. Until then, stay out of my affairs.'' Lindy regretted the harsh words the minute they tumbled over her tongue. Steve looked at her as though she'd stabbed a knife into his chest. A muscle in his jaw leaped to life and she saw her brother mentally withdrawing from her, as if a mechanical door were slowly lowering, blocking her out.

His eyes narrowed and hardened as his angry gaze briefly met hers. "If that's the way you want it."

It wasn't, but she didn't know how to retract those cruel words. He didn't bother to wait for an answer and marched away from her. Lindy caught up with him in the baggage claim area and they rode into the city in a stilted, uneasy silence.

"I didn't mean what I said earlier," Lindy told him, once they were inside the apartment.

Her brother didn't look at her. "Yes, you did," he said after a moment, and walked away from her.

"I seem to be batting a thousand lately," Lindy confided to Susan. She'd been back from Hawaii almost three weeks now, but this was the first opportunity she'd had to visit her friend. "In one short week, I managed to alienate both my husband and my brother."

"Have you heard from Rush?" Susan asked, replenishing the coffee in both their cups.

"No. But then I didn't expect to."

"Have you written him?"

Lindy reached for her coffee cup, cradling it with both hands, letting the warmth burn her palms. "No."

Susan pulled out a chair and slumped down. She was nearly five months pregnant and just starting to wear maternity tops. She looked soft and fragile, but underneath she was as tough as leather. Lindy would have given everything she owned to possess the same grit and fortitude as her friend.

"From what I can tell, you've put yourself in a no-win situation," Susan said softly, sadly.

"My God, Rush was nearly killed. It was so close. The doctors said—" Lindy paused and bit into her bottom lip to control the emotion that rocked her every time she thought about the accident.

"He could have gotten hurt in a car accident driving to an office just as easily. Would you suggest he never sit in a car again?"

"No. Of course not." Her hands shook as she raised the mug to her lips and took a sip. "The accident taught me something more. Whatever it takes to be a good navy wife, I don't have it. I couldn't stand on that pier and smile the next time Rush gleefully sails off into the sunset. I can't take these long months of separation. I always thought married people were one, a unit, two people sculpting a life together. It's not that way with Rush. It won't ever be that way—not as long as he's in the navy. I can't be like you, Susan. I wish I could, but it's just not in me."

"You'd rather be separated for a lifetime?" Susan questioned, frowning.

"Yes. It would be easier than dying by inches. No. Oh God, Susan, I don't know what I want anymore."

Her friend didn't say anything for a long time, and when she did, her voice was gentle, understanding. "I stopped counting the times I've said goodbye to Jeff a long time ago. Every time I stand out on that pier and watch that huge carrier pull away, I think I'll never be able to do it again. Letting Jeff go, and doing it with a smile, takes everything there is inside me. You've got it wrong, Lindy. You think I'm so brave and good, but I'm not."

"But you are."

"No. I'm just a woman who loves her man."

"I love Rush, too," Lindy returned defiantly.

"I know, and he loves you." The tip of Susan's finger circled the rim of her coffee cup as she averted her gaze, her look thoughtful. "I don't think I'll ever forget the night I first met you. We were in the kitchen chatting, and Rush and Jeff were fiddling around on the patio with the barbecue. Remember?"

Lindy nodded.

"You were holding one of the boys and I saw Rush look at you. Lindy, there's no way I can describe the longing that came into his eyes. Just watching him stare at you with such tenderness made me want to weep. It was as if you were the Madonna holding the baby Jesus. In that moment, I knew how much your love had changed Rush, and how important you had become to him in those short weeks.

"You might succeed in getting him to leave the

navy, but in time you'll regret it. I know Rush will. Eventually it would cripple him, and in the process, you. If ever there was a man who was meant to lead others, meant to serve his country, it's Rush.''

"Why is it always the woman who has to change?" Lindy cried. "It's not fair."

"You're right," Susan agreed, with a sad smile. "It isn't fair. All I can say is, if you try to change Rush and succeed, he won't be the same man you fell in love with, or the same man you married."

Lindy bowed her head, more confused than ever.

"Rush took your words to heart," Susan added, looking both disheartened and disappointed.

Lindy jerked her gaze up. "How do you know that?"

"He doesn't expect you to be waiting for him when the *Mitchell* docks next month. Jeff wrote that Rush has volunteered for the first watch."

"What does that mean?"

"It means he's going to remain on board as officer of the day the first twelve hours after the crew is dismissed. He told Jeff he didn't have any reason to hurry home since you weren't going to be there."

"But, I didn't mean I wouldn't be at the apartment!"

Susan shrugged. "How was Rush supposed to know that?"

The phone rang twice and Lindy glanced at her watch, calculating if she had enough time to answer it before meeting Susan and the other navy wives. She had no intention of being late for this last fling before the *Mitchell* docked. Taking a chance, she hurried into the kitchen.

"All right, all right," she grumbled, and reached for the receiver. "Hello?"

Her greeting was followed by a short silence, and then a soft female voice asked, "Is Steve Kyle available, please?"

"Carol? Is that you?" Lindy's heart started to pound with excitement. She'd been wanting to talk to her former sister-in-law for weeks.

"Who's this?"

Carol's voice was far from fragile and she could almost picture the petite, gentle blonde squaring her shoulders and bringing up her chin.

"It's Lindy."

"Lindy! I didn't know you were in Seattle."

"Six months now."

"You should have called. I'd love to see you again."

"I wanted to contact you," Lindy said, her spirits lifting as a Christmas song came over the radio, "but Steve wasn't in favor of the idea. How are you?"

"Good. Real good. Well, tell me—are you Mrs. Paul Abrams yet?" The question was followed by a light, infectious laugh. "The last time I saw you,

Paul had just given you a diamond ring and you were floating on cloud nine.''

It was difficult for Lindy to remember those days. She may have been fooled into thinking she was happy, but that contentment had been short-lived. She would never have been the right woman for Paul. Once again she thanked God he'd had enough foresight to have recognized as much.

"I married Rush Callaghan," Lindy told her.

A short, shocked silence followed. "You did? Why that's wonderful—congratulations. I've always had a soft spot in my heart for Rush."

The last person Lindy wanted to discuss was her husband, especially the way matters were between them now. "Steve isn't here at the moment, but he'll be back soon. I'll tell him you called." Lindy hesitated and then decided she couldn't hold her tongue any longer. "I don't know what happened between you two—Steve never told me—but whatever it is, I hope you can patch it up. He misses you dreadfully." Lindy knew her brother would have her hide if he knew she'd told Carol that.

Carol laughed, but the mirth couldn't disguise her pain. "He's gotten along fine without me, and I've learned to manage without him, too. Leave a message for him, will you?"

"Of course."

"But tell him—" Carol added quickly, "—tell him it isn't overly important."

"Sure. I'll be happy to."

"It was nice talking to you again, Lindy. Really nice. I'm pleased for you and Rush. Be happy, you hear?"

Lindy nodded, although she knew Carol couldn't see the action. "I will," she mumbled. "I will."

Rush stood at the bridge ready to be relieved of duty. The sky was a deep shade of pearl gray and he expected it to start raining any minute. The foul weather suited his mood. The *Mitchell* was home, and his friends had hurried off the carrier and down the gangway to a happy reunion with their wives and families, eager to spend the holidays with their loved ones.

Rush had stood on the bridge, hungrily scanning the crowds through his binoculars, hoping with everything in him that he'd find Lindy there. He would have given his retirement pay to have found her among the well-wishers, waiting for him.

But Lindy hadn't been there, and a small part of Rush had died with the knowledge. Cheryl hadn't been there for him, either. Rush shouldn't have been surprised. Lindy had told him in Hawaii she had no intention of standing on the gangway, and she'd meant it. He was a fool to even have expected her.

His watchful gaze scanned the outline of the city of Bremerton and the Christmas decorations that hung from the streetlights. For the past six weeks of the cruise, he'd closed himself off from thoughts of Lindy, mentally chastising himself for exposing his heart a second time. Over and over again, he'd told himself women were too fickle to be trusted. But now that he was in port everything had changed and he knew he would eventually have to face her.

Marrying Lindy had been a gamble—he'd known it the day he slipped the wedding band on her finger. Her brother had had every reason to come down on him so hard. His friend was right. Rush had taken advantage of Lindy. He'd cashed in on her pain and insecurities, used her infatuation with him for his own purposes. It wasn't any wonder Lindy was confused and miserably unhappy now. Everything that had happened between them was his fault and he accepted full responsibility. Lindy wasn't ready to be a wife and she wanted out.

Rush didn't blame her.

His relief arrived and, after making the necessary notations in the log, Rush picked up his seabag and headed down the steep gangway. A stiff, cold breeze hit him and he paused to raise the collar of his thick wool jacket. There was no reason to hurry, and his steps were heavy.

His left arm was free of the cast now, but he still hadn't regained full use of it. His shoulder ached almost unbearably at times, but Rush had welcomed the pain. The physical throbbing somehow helped overshadow the mental agony of what had happened between him and Lindy.

Halfway down the gangway, something made him glance up. He stopped, his heart thundering against his rib cage, unable to believe his own eyes. There, alone at the end of the pier stood Lindy. The strong wind plastered her long coat to her torso and beat her thick dark hair roughly about her face. Her hands were buried in her coat pockets and she'd raised her chin, her loving eyes following his movements, patiently waiting.

Years of discipline, weeks of control, snapped within Rush as he dropped his seabag and started walking toward her. His chest felt as though he was on fire, he was fighting so hard to bury the emotion that pounded through him. His pulse started to beat in his temple. She'd come. His Lindy had come.

Rush quickened his pace and Lindy started running toward him, her arms outstretched. He caught her and pulled her into his embrace, burying his face in her soft hair, breathing in her delicate scent.

He tried to speak and found he couldn't. His tongue might as well have been attached to the roof of his mouth, and after a half second, he gave up trying to voice his thoughts. It came to him then how unnecessary words really were.

He sighed and reveled in the warm glow of Lindy's love at full strength. It worked on him like a healing potion, a relentless tide surging against him at full crest. It was as though they had exchanged their wedding vows there, at that moment on that pier, so strong was the love that flowed between them.

"Rush," she cried, tears in her voice. "I'm sorry, so sorry."

She held him so tightly that Rush could barely breathe. He closed his eyes, letting his heart and mind soak up her words. Each one tenderly removed the barbs of doubt that had tormented him, each one healed the pain and deep sense of loss these past weeks of separation had brought him. Each word confirmed what he'd always known but had been afraid to admit, fearing it would cripple him for life. He loved Lindy, loved her beyond anything else there could ever be in his world. He loved her more than the thrill of navigating the oceans, more than serving his country and commanding men. From the minute she'd given him her heart, Rush had only one mistress, only one wife, and that was Lindy.

"I love you," she said fiercely. "I've been such a fool." Lindy felt home at last in Rush's arms. This was where she belonged, where she planned to stay. It had taken these long weeks apart for her to realize what a fool she'd been to risk losing this wonderful man. Everything Susan had said was true, and Lindy had finally recognized the truth in her friend's words.

"You?" His voice was strained and husky with

emotion. "If anyone was a fool, it was me. I should never have walked away from you in Hawaii."

The muscles in his lean jaw bunched and she kissed him, not able to wait a moment longer. Her hands lovingly stroked the sides of his face, relishing touching him so freely. Her mind groped for the words to explain.

"I was wrong, Rush, so wrong to try to force you to choose between me and the navy."

"Lindy, stop." He held a hand to her mouth to cut off her words. "Listen to me, my love. The reenlistment papers are in my pocket. I haven't signed them, and I won't."

She broke away, her face tight with disbelief. "You most certainly will sign those papers, Rush Callaghan."

From the look he gave her, Lindy knew she couldn't have shocked him more had she announced she was six months pregnant. His gaze narrowed as he studied her.

"The last time we talked, you were dead set against the navy. You wanted to be first in my life. I'm telling you I'm willing to give you what you want."

"You came so close to dying," she reminded him softly, and her voice trembled slightly with remembered pain. "I don't know if you're even aware of how badly you were injured."

He shook his head.

Rush had changed in so many ways since Hawaii. His shoulders were broader and his eyes less clouded, letting her look into his heart and know his thoughts.

"I couldn't bear the thought of losing you, Rush. It terrified me. I decided that if I was going to be forced to give you up, I'd rather get it over with quickly instead of letting go of you a little at a time. That was why I asked you to give up the navy. That was why I told you I wouldn't be here when you returned. Believe me, I know how crazy that sounds now. But at the time I felt I was doing the right thing."

"That's the most twisted piece of reasoning I've ever heard."

"I know," she whispered, dropping her gaze.

"Lindy, I meant what I said about those reenlistment papers. If you want a civilian for a husband, I'll do my damnedest to adjust."

She met his intense gaze and smiled through her tears. "Sign the papers, Rush. I've done a lot of maturing these past six weeks. You wanted a navy wife and by God, you've got one."

He stared at her and a strange, unidentifiable light flared in his gaze, darkening and then lightening their cornflower blue.

"You mean it, don't you?"

She nodded vigorously. "You bet I do. I may

make mistakes along the way, but I'm willing to learn. I love you, Rush.''

"I love you, wife."

"Navy wife," she amended.

Rush laughed and folded her in his arms, holding on to her as though he never planned to let her go. When they broke apart, Rush retrieved his seabag, and with their arms wrapped around each other's waists, they stepped forward toward tomorrow—a naval officer and his first mate.

* * * * *

But what about Steve and Carol?
Don't miss their story this June in

DEBBIE MACOMBER'S

Here's a sneak peek...

Seducing her ex-husband wasn't going to be easy,
Carol Kyle decided, but she was determined. More than
determined—resolute! Her mind was set, and no one knew
better than Steve Kyle how stubborn she could be when
she wanted something.

And Carol wanted a baby.

Naturally she had no intention of letting him in on
her plans. What he didn't know wouldn't hurt him. Their
marriage had lasted five good years, and six bad months.
To Carol's way of thinking, which she admitted was a bit
twisted at the moment, Steve owed her at least one pregnancy.

Turning thirty had convinced Carol that drastic measures
were necessary. Her hormones were jumping up and down,
screaming for a chance at motherhood. Her biological
clock was ticking away, and Carol swore she could hear
every beat of that blasted timepiece. It was when she found
herself wandering through the infant section of her favorite
department store that she realized extreme measures
needed to be taken.

Making the initial contact with Steve hadn't been easy, but she recognized that the first move had to come from her. Getting in touch with her ex-husband after more than a year of complete silence had required two weeks of nerve building. But she'd managed to swallow her considerable pride and do it.

Carol needed him for only one tempestuous night, and then, if everything went according to schedule, Steve Kyle could fade out of her life once more. If she failed to get pregnant...well, she'd leap that hurdle when she came to it.

**Will Carol get her ex-husband—
and get pregnant?
Don't miss the exciting story in**

Available this June.

Where love comes alive™

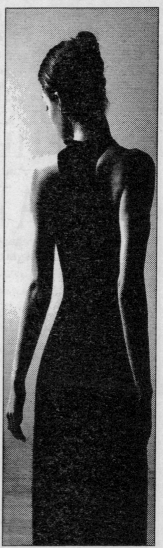